SECRETS OF A SUPERTHIEF

D1557232

JACK MACLEAN
SECRETS OF A
SUPERTHIEF

EDITED, WITH AN INTRODUCTION BY TOM ZITO, *WASHINGTON POST*

ILLUSTRATED BY BRUCE PETUSH

BERKLEY BOOKS, NEW YORK

SECRETS OF A SUPERTHIEF

A Berkley Book / published by arrangement with
the author

PRINTING HISTORY
Berkley trade paperback edition / May 1983

All right reserved.
Copyright © 1983 by Superthief Enterprises, Inc.

This book may not be reproduced in whole or in part,
by mimeograph or any other means, without permission.
For information address: Berkley Publishing Corporation,
200 Madison Avenue, New York, New York 10016.

ISBN: 0-425-05645-7

A BERKLEY BOOK® TM 757,375

The name "BERKLEY" and the stylized "B" with design are
trademarks belonging to Berkley Publishing Corporation.

PRINTED IN THE UNITED STATES OF AMERICA

HENNEPIN COUNTY LIBRARY

JUN 2 9 1983   9

For My Parents

Contents

Introduction

FORT LAUDERDALE, Florida, March 3l, Reu-
ters—Superthief Jack MacLean began a 15-year
prison term today for hundreds of burglaries that
netted him 133 million dollars' worth of jewels—
and at least one detective found that "kind of sad"
to see. Detective Arthur McLellan, MacLean's
nemesis, explained:

"I enjoyed working against such a pro. He's a
Superthief... an electronics genius with an IQ of
167 and to top it all, he didn't believe in violence.
He never carried a gun..."

This wire story wound up on my editor's desk at The *Washington Post* in spring of 1980, and I spent the next month learning everything I could about Jack MacLean.

He had never called himself Superthief—that was an appellation cops and robbers had used to define this legend they knew so little about. He worked alone, stole solely from the rich, never harmed the houses he hit—not so much as a door jamb or a flower bed—and always reset burglar alarms. He owned a Hughes 300C helicopter equipped with pontoons, a Lake seaplane, a Cessna 172 modified to carry a trail bike, a $40,000 Scarab high-speed boat and several fast cars and motorcycles.

Jack MacLean was a dream subject for a newspaper profile. In the course of his work, he encountered pet monkeys, armadillos, a bobcat in a cage, skunks, owls, inflatable dolls and even another burglar, about to break a window and set off an alarm. "Stop, thief," he yelled, and the man ran away. It was almost too good to be true, as if I was dealing with a real-life version of the Cary Grant in *To Catch a Thief,* or Raffles, the Victorian second-story man. Jack was good-looking (as an infant he had appeared in Mullins Baby Food ads), smart and funny. He stole an abandoned puppy (a mistreated one from down the street, which he named Swag—police jargon for stolen goods), diamonds and the hearts of women with equal ease. And although he was a criminal (albeit a new one; he had no record other than a long list of speeding tickets), he had a heart as big as the Ritz.

On one occasion, he slipped out of a house he had just hit, only to spy a young boy badly hurt from a fall on a bike. The black-clad burglar slipped behind a bush, donned the white change of clothing he always carried in his emergency pouch, and told the boy to hang on while he called for help. He ran back to the just-burgled house, once again disconnected the alarm system, and stole inside to phone the police. He left the house and reset the alarm—one of his classic characteristics.

"I would never want some punk to be able to walk into a house I had just hit and make a mess of the place," he told me.

He had the wit of an outlaw Woody Allen and an encyclopedic knowledge of burglar alarms, which he constantly updated. After being foiled several times by a particular system, he tore one out of a house and dragged it home to master its workings.

Superthief's most legendary trait was his ability to use the hardware, the dialogue and the procedures of law enforcement to outsleuth the police. He had the same equipment, but better maintained; the same skills, but more finely honed; the same mentality, but shifted from a defensive to an offensive position.

And so it was that he could fly in his helicopter and use police lingo and police radios to access the Federal stolen goods computer network. He would wait until a month or two after a job to check on whether particular items had been reported stolen. If they had not been, he would keep or sell them; if they had been, he would swing out over the ocean and deep six the potential evidence.

He studied the police with a schoolboy fascination, the way the police might dream of studying criminals. At times this entailed photographing police activities, simply to discover the mistakes they made. On another occasion, he staked out a stakeout, conversing with the cops by radio as if he were part of the pack. On one evening when he was not busy working, he followed an FBI agent into a Burger King. The agent himself was following a suspect, and when their eyes locked, Superthief said to the agent: "Nice night for a stakeout...I mean a steak dinner out."

If he consistently displayed a sharp sense of wit, it was partly because he perceived the roles of cop and criminal to incorporate much of the art of a professional actor.

One night—a particular December 23, to be specific—he was drilling through the garage door of a family whose next-door neighbors were hosting a huge Christmas party. Cars were parked all over the neighborhood, and a late arrival pulled into the driveway where Superthief was working.

He put his tools down and walked up to the driver.

"I'm sorry," he said calmly. "But these people don't want anyone parking here." The car drove off.

Such was his sense of humor. He would glue old sets of dentures to doorknobs, short-sheet beds, empty self-defense weapons found in drawers and leave them—chambers open—arranged in symmetrical rows in conspicuous places. If he considered the amount of jewelry he found too insignificant or insulting to take, he would set the gems on the kitchen table and steal the control panel of the victim's burglar alarm instead. He often left telephone books open to the appropriate page, the police department listing circled with the notation, "Call this number."

"I didn't want people to take this too seriously," he told me. "I wanted them to be able to laugh in the midst of their misfortune."

Jack is in jail now. He violated one of his own key rules—never to have an accomplice on the scene of a crime—and he was caught. As the cops went through his home on the day of his arrest, they headed for the bedroom. "Hold it! There are dogs in there," he yelled. The cops froze in their tracks, reaching for their guns. Jack opened the door, and four tiny poodles marched out.

"What's this dog's name?" one of the cops asked.

"Swag," Jack said. "I stole him."

About twenty-five kids from the neighborhood were in court the day of his sentencing. They seemed shocked as the bailiff slipped a set of hand-cuffs over the defendant's wrists—even more so when he turned to them and said:

"I want you kids to see this as proof that crime doesn't pay."

Jack has changed now, but he hasn't forgotten what it was like to be in the words of Detective McLellan, "the most successful burglar in history." It takes a thief to foil a thief. And Superthief Jack MacLean has a lot of super insights to share in this book.

TOM ZITO
Loudoun County, Virginia
March 1982

Preface

Picture this: you're at home watching television, washing the dishes, or getting changed in the bedroom—only to discover a stranger peering through your window.

Who is it? Could it be an itinerant prowler? The Peeping Tom down the street? Or is a burglar getting ready to break in for your cash or jewelry? If it is, did he see you? Does he know that you're home?

More specifically, what are you going to do if you're in your apartment, mobile home, regular home or any place of residence and somebody is

1

breaking in? Naturally you're going to run for the phone! But what if that phone line is dead? Now what? What are you going to do now?

By the time you finish reading this book, you'll know exactly what to do...and have learned a lot about how to avoid getting into this kind of predicament in the first place.

I was an expert at burglary—until I made the mistake of working with some people who weren't as meticulous as I was...and now I am in prison writing this book.

My main purpose in writing is to prevent residential crime. I have written in plain and simple language, easy for anybody to understand. No big fancy words, or difficult theories to comprehend. I've done it this way, because if there's anything I hate, it's needing a dictionary beside a book I read, or an attorney sitting next to me to translate legal scripture.

Why are burglaries on the increase today, with all these crime-prevention and neighborhood-watch programs going on, and all the new heavy-duty locks and invincible burglar alarm systems that are on the market now? Why are all these not reducing the number of burglaries?

One aspect is that every so-called crime-prevention program—either put on by police departments or the Crime-Watch people themselves—is conceived in the wrong way. Burglary is a mind game, played by people who are using their heads to decide whether or not to hit your house. Hundreds of considerations run through a burglar's mind, and he either says to himself and his accomplices, "Let's go for it," or "Pass."

But today's crime programs are trying to match heavy-duty locks against muscles and tools. The lock companies are making heavier locks, with longer deadbolts. And you know what that does to a burglar's way of thinking? It makes him go to the nearest hardware store to replace his one-foot crowbar with a four-foot crowbar. And when the lock company puts larger lock casings on their so-called burglar-proof deadbolts, it makes a burglar exchange his nine-inch pair of channel lock pliers for a twenty-four-inch pair of channel locks that will grab and take off any deadbolt around. So you say, sure...but who goes around carrying tools like that?

I've got a better question for you. How many assaults like this will your home be able to survive, and do you want to take the chance even if there aren't many burglars running around with tools of that caliber? Before I became a burglar, I was a licensed locksmith in a major city for three years. And in those three years I heard time and time again from my customers these typical phrases: "Oh, we don't have any problems around here. Mrs. Brown from down the street keeps an eye on the house when we're gone." That's the biggest joke I've heard in my life. Do any of you watch a neighbor's home for them and, if so, how many seconds in a week do you watch it out of the 604,800 that tick by? And can you watch all sides of it from where you live? Let's face it. Watching homes for people is nothing but a waste of time.

Here's another beauty: "Oh, burglars wouldn't dare hit our neighborhood. There's a policeman living right across the street." When I was working areas in my earlier days where policemen lived, I'd hit the houses on both sides of his and across the street, and then leave a note on the police car windshield, saying, "Keep up the good work."

BURGLARY IS A PSYCHOLOGICAL GAME. It's a burglar's brains and wits against your home's heavy-duty locks and doors. Don't overpower burglars with hardware when you should be playing *mind games* with him. Play with a burglar's head. That's what this book is all about: how to dress up your home with inexpensive items that will have the burglar running in the other direction. Outwit him with mind-deterring scare tactics, NOT overpowering hardware.

Don't get me wrong. Hardware is good, and I'm going to tell you what kind of locks and doors and windows are best, and what type of alarm systems are most efficient. But if you'll use 70 percent mind games and 30 percent hardware as your wall of defense, you'll come out much more secure in the end.

Part of this book is based on the things that deterred me from different homes, that made me say, "Oh hell... next door has got to be easier." But then a person could say, "Well, just because a certain thing scared you off... doesn't mean that it would scare off another burglar." That's a good point. But believe me, I had the gall of twenty and the guts to back it up. If it deterred me, it surely would deter someone else. But how many? How many other burglars would be scared away by the same things that scared me away?

That bothered me to the point that while in prison I decided to put together a survey for use in the crime-prevention programs I would be putting on when I got out. And in that survey, I felt I could find out just how many burglars got scared off by this or that. I sat down one day and, with the help of a few other burglars and one or two guards, came up with 129 questions covering every aspect of residential crime. Then I gave it to 300 inmates put in prison for the crime of burglary and other residential crimes.

To my knowledge there has never been a survey given in a prison by another inmate on a volunteer basis. I have however heard of a few surveys given by police to people who have just been arrested. As a matter of fact I don't think the police called their line of questioning a survey, as much as they called the results a survey. They arrived at the results by questioning people right after they were arrested— about subjects connected with the cases they would be tried for! (And take it from me, when you've just been arrested, you don't know what the hell is going on.) Then the police put together a few answers from this one and a few answers from that one and call it a survey. That's like ten people coming to your house, each with one flower, and as the tenth one is added to the other nine, you decide to call it a bouquet. If there ever were surveys given by law enforcement agencies to known burglars, I get the general impression, from the way the inmates feel about the police, that the surveys couldn't have been conducted in very comfortable situations or led to very honest responses. The subject has to feel relaxed and trusting and unhurried in order for a survey to be meaningful. We had nothing but time on our hands, and nowhere to go.

Before asking the questions, I informed the inmates that names and numbers were not important, only truthful answers. And I told them that there was absolutely nothing they could say that would impress me, either in amounts of valuables taken, or a method of breaking in. The survey accomplished two things more than anything: it showed that the same mind deterrents that scared me away would scare other burglars away; and it pinpointed weak areas in homes that need protection.

In the survey I asked these other men about the tools of their trade, where they would look for the goods, and the ways they preferred getting in. Which times were best for them and worst for you? What were their methods and procedures? What would stop them? As a result of this survey, you're not just going to reap the benefits of Superthief's experiences. You're going to know the M.O.s of a whole prison population of burglars and thieves.

I am going to stress, throughout the book, the importance of putting together the right combination of deterrents, on and around your home, to make burglars and thieves want to go elsewhere. It's like a combination lock. A combination lock, as we all know, works on a series of preselected numbers that, when put into the right order, open the lock. If the lock has ninety-nine numbers that need to be put into the correct order, and you use only ninety-eight of them, the lock isn't going to open. You *must* use all of the numbers in order to get the results that you want. And it's the same thing with my crime protection program. There are many, many things that you can do, but *you should do all of them* to get the safest and best results.

I can't stress too much here that many of these deterrents are psychological games—mental deterrents you'll have to play on prospective burglars. Remember, it takes a thief to foil a thief. I know what would have kept me away. The inmates told me what frightened them. And I'm going to share my insights with you in this book.

CHAPTER 1

KNOW THY ENEMY

If, as we've said, burglary is a mind game, then you've got to understand who it is you're up against so you can outwit him. By describing for you profiles of four typical types of burglars, you'll get a good idea of the various M.O.s that are being used against you. And although I'll point out specific things you can do about this later in the book, it's important for you to begin thinking about ways to foil each of these characters.

The Amateur

The most common kind of burglar is the third-class amateur, who is usually between the ages of fifteen and twenty-two and uses any hand tool he has to break into a home. He—although I should emphasize that there are female burglars in all these categories—generally does a lot of damage getting in, stays away from homes with alarm systems, and is often using drugs while he works. In fact, drugs are often the principal thing this category of burglar is after, followed by money, jewelry, stereos, televisions, etc. The amateur works by day or night, usually uses his own personal vehicle for transportation, and tends to be accompanied by friends, who also are often using drugs.

The Self-Claimed Professional

The second most common class of burglar is usually between the ages of twenty-three and thirty, and carries crowbars, channel locks, screwdrivers, credit cards, knives and any other sort of hand tool. Although he will tend to stay away from homes with alarm systems, on occasion he will attempt to bypass the system—i.e., break into the house without turning the system off—by, for example, cutting a piece of glass without upsetting the alarm foil tape on a window.

The self-proclaimed professional is mainly after jewelry and silver, as well as money and drugs. He works by day or night, and often will pose as a delivery man, meter reader, repair man or garbage collector if working by day. This class of burglar almost always has acting capabilities, and doesn't mind confronting people. His self-confidence has been highly developed through the execution of successful burglaries and he has little fear of being caught. He generally uses gloves. If he uses electronics—radios or police scanners—they are generally of cheap quality. He usually drives his own vehicle, sometimes parking right in the driveway of a home being burglarized.

Just A Kid

This fourth-class burglar, who can be anywhere from seven to fourteen, is the third most common type on the street. He'll carry a screwdriver, knife, stick or rock, and generally gets involved in shoplifting, yard pilferage, open-garage theft and residential breaking and entering, although he usually avoids force by crawling through openings.

The kid in question here is after money and radios, TVs, stereos—anything he is capable of carrying. Sometimes he looks for drugs. He almost always operates by daylight, travels by foot or bike, and rarely uses gloves—unless he's seen a lot of cops and robbers programs.

Extreme Professional

This is an extremely rare category of burglar, by far the most clever of the lot, and also by far the least common. Permit me to be immodest and say this was the category Superthief fell into. Because of the expertise and mentality needed to be an extreme professional, it is rare to find someone under the age of thirty in this class. He will carry lock picks for both doors and alarms, channel locks, a crowbar and a screwdriver.

The extreme professional can—by way of picking or other means—shut off complete alarm systems. Only on very rare occasions will he bypass a system. He might, for example, crawl under an electric-eye beam. He can pick open most door locks, can climb well, run fast and tends to be thin and agile, so he can ease himself through small spaces.

Unlike all other burglars, he will not take TVs, radios, stereos, furniture and other heavy objects—although on occasion he may walk off with a small safe that looks too good to pass up. He is mainly interested in money, jewelry, silver, paintings, stamp collections, coin collections, and other small valuables.

This first-class burglar will:

- Not confront anyone ever or let anyone see him

- Not carry weapons of any kind

- Not work between hours other than 6 P.M. to 10 P.M., which is when most people tend to go out

- Not use a vehicle to go from place to place, but rather will be dropped off and walk to his work site

- Not work with anyone on the scene

- Not tell friends of his burglaries

- Not forget to wear gloves

- Never work in daylight hours

- Never break his own rules.

The extreme professional has spent much time studying law enforcement procedures and technology, and knows police codes, frequencies, lingo, cars, and the size of their force. He will monitor them on sophisticated electric equipment with descramblers, if necessary, and use FM radios—not C.B.s—for his own communications. He will know police procedures so well that, when the police themselves are aware that he is monitoring them and have, in advance, set up alternate radio procedures and frequencies, he will be able to tell by radio transmissions that something is wrong and will pay closer attention to other channels.

This first-class burglar will have catlike proximity awareness, excellent sight and hearing, and fear little. He will wear long pants and long-sleeved shirts to prevent getting cut or scraped. From the time he leaves his own house he will trust no one. If something moves, it's a cop. If he hears a dog, it's a police dog. If he runs into a tree, it's a police tree.

Now let's hear what some of the other inmates had to say about burglars in general:

Why did you do burglaries?

A. Eighty percent said that they did burglaries for the money they gained from it. This includes anything they would take: jewelry, stereos, TVs—all sold to bring a buck. Twelve percent said that they did it for the excitement, while the other 8 percent said that they did it for revenge: the girlfriend moves in with another guy, taking half of his possessions with her; or the wife divorces the husband and winds up with everything. A guy who hit one house nine times did it because he was fired from his job. It was his boss's house. I've heard this from several of the inmates: when they were fired, they were so mad that they hit the boss's house. Bosses: Have you been burglarized lately? If so, have you fired anybody or had a particularly bad time with anybody at work? Watch out for this. It does happen more than you think. It would be a safe guess to state that if you have fired a guy who is a sideline burglar, he will hit your house. What makes it worse is that the fired employee knows your schedule well.

At what age did you start doing burglaries?

A. Sixty-seven percent of the 300 inmates given this survey said that they started burglaries between the ages of eleven and fifteen. Fifty percent stated that their parents knew about it. Sixty-three percent said their parents did nothing to stop them.

Twenty-eight percent said that they started burglaries between the ages of sixteen and twenty-one, and the remaining 5 percent were between five and ten years old. I started burglaries in my late twenties.

Did you do burglaries for a living?

A. Only 35 percent of the inmates did burglaries for a living! The other 65 percent supplemented their burglaries with other jobs, selling drugs, etc.

Do you in your own mind think that you are a professional?

A. Only 25 percent thought they were professionals in the sense of being very good at it, while the other 75 percent knew they weren't. I talked to only one inmate out of the 300 who I thought was 10 percent on his way to being good.

Did you do crimes other than burglaries?

A. Eighty-five percent of the inmates said that they did commit other crimes along with burglary. Fifteen percent said they did not. I didn't pursue the issue any further than a yes or no, fearing that they might think I was working for the police, digging up evidence of other crimes they'd committed. What they did think about the purpose of my survey is exactly what I intended it for: crime-prevention programs and this book. They all knew it and didn't mind taking it.

Have you ever been to prison before for burglary?

A. Sixty-four percent said that they had been imprisoned before for burglary or other crime. The other 36 percent stated that this was their first experience of incarceration. However, many of them had been on probation.

Have you learned from prison life how to commit more and different kinds of crime?

A. Ninety-five percent stated that they have learned many more kinds of crime while being in prison.

Would you agree that a good name for prison would be the College of Better Crime Education?

A. The same results were obtained on this question, with 95 percent agreeing that prisons are schools for taking vacations and learning more methods of crime. One day I overheard another inmate ticking off various ways of blowing up vehicles in ninety seconds. The inmates who heard him are now mentally equipped to blow up any vehicle on the streets. Whether they will retain this information by the time they are released is another question.

Prisons are places where inmates can get together and tell stories of all kinds—including tales of the crimes they've pulled off—and teach others new and improved methods. They explain how they were caught, and the next guy learns from the other's mistakes, so he won't make the same one, when he gets out. They exchange mistakes, improving their ways so that they build up false courage, thinking they're much better than when they came in. And they can't wait to get out to practice their new methods. I've been asked by literally hundreds of inmates about my methods and ways to do this and that: how I shut off alarms, etc. Needless to say, they have learned nothing from me, except that it was a waste of time to ask.

Now that you've been to prison, when you get out would further prison time deter you from doing more burglaries?

A. OK . . . place your bets. Do you think prison is a deterrent or not? Let me give you a few hints. While in prison there was a guy whose locker was broken into seven times. He lost over ninety-five dollars and one watch, plus various other things. Need more hints? One day in the laundry, one of the laundry inmates who had access to sheets stole them and sold extra ones for fifty cents apiece to other inmates. For what? Who knows? Probably for smoking. They smoked everything else around there. Seventy percent admitted to me that they were going to continue burglaries and other crimes, when they get out. And you know what the general attitude was about it all? They knew their mistakes now and they were not going to make them again. They've improved their systems and techniques. The other 30 percent said that they were pretty sure that they weren't going to do any more burglaries.

Would you ever portray a service man when doing a burglary?

A. This mainly applies to daytime burglaries. Fifty-five percent said that they have appeared at the door of a home as a lawn maintenance man, meter reader, salesman or any other of the many possible positions to be portrayed. The other 45 percent do only nighttime burglaries and this wouldn't apply to them. This is a serious problem. Make sure any service person approaching your home has a proper I.D. If in doubt, don't let him in without calling whomever he claims to represent.

Do you carry weapons?

A. Fifty percent said yes, they carried either guns or knives. (I never carried a weapon.) But to be on the safe side, should you ever come in contact with a burglar, consider him armed and extremely dangerous, especially when caught in a house with no way out. His only way of survival is to fight, and he will more than likely be out of control, high on drugs, and should not be approached in any way, other than by police at gunpoint. If you ever come home and find a door ajar, a window slightly opened that you left closed, or other signs of something wrong that you can't account for at that second, turn right around and walk back to your car, or to a neighbor's house and call the police. Gentlemen, never let your anger or tenth-degree black belt in karate make you think your body won't accept bullets as well as the next body will. Call the police, even if you think no one is in the house. If you are wrong, you may not live to tell about it.

Did you use radios of any kind while doing your burglaries?

A. Thirty percent said they used C.B. walkie talkies. Knowing how jumbled up the channels are today, that must have been fun. I can hear them now: "Hey Fred...the coast is clear....Where are you?...Breaker Breaker good buddy. ...What's your handle?...Fred, is that you?...You say your handle is Fred.... How original, mine's the Rubber Duck. ...Fred, where the hell are you?...Hey, listen buddy, you don't have to swear about it....Hey, Joe...I got the gold.... Where should I go?...What do you mean I'm old....Why you young whipper snappers....Hey, Joe, don't speak to that guy....He's using the C.B. for a hobby." Those must have been some pretty professional burglaries, or at least some pretty comical ones.

On the serious side...burglars today are using radios more and more for burglary and other crimes from what I was told during the survey. Should you see anyone running around with radios, looking suspicious, use your own judgment. Call the police if you think they are up to something.

Do you have anybody working on the scene with you while doing burglaries?

A. Eighty-eight percent said they used a partner, either male or female, working with them right at the house. The other 12 percent were, like I was, doing the jobs alone.

How near your own home do you do burglaries?

A. Fifty-one percent said that they go at least five miles away from home to do the burglaries. So it doesn't always have to be the kid next door. However, 30 percent said that they work less than a half-mile from home, so don't rule out the kid down the street. One inmate told me that he hit the lady's house right next door to his at least four times—and how convenient it was because he could watch her leave the house. The other 19 percent said they worked at least three miles away from their residence.

Do you prefer burglarizing houses, apartments, condominiums or motels/ hotels?

A. Houses and townhouses received first choice with 69 percent saying that they were the easiest and safest to burglarize and get away from. Second choice was condominiums with 19 percent, while

10 percent stated that they specialized in apartments. The remaining 2 percent went to hotels/motels. The fact is, burglary can happen anyplace and to anything. When I was in jail, four guys broke into the jail to get a few inmates out. They pulled it off, but were all caught days later—and wound up spending a nice long time in the same place they had spent three days breaking into. I've heard of being in a hurry to get someplace, but...

Did you stake out (case) places before you hit them?

A. Eighty-five percent of the inmates said they did case out whatever they were going to burglarize, while 15 percent said they just hit them at random. My viewpoint: Casing out places was TV stuff, a waste of time, dangerous and not necessary. But if you see anyone hanging around and feel they are watching your home or business, the police will be more than happy to check for you. Remember what the person or car looked like, and write down any identifying details so that the police will have enough to work with. Give the information over the phone so the police can dispatch descriptions to their patrol cars. The more information you can give the police, the better their chances of helping you. When in doubt—call the police.

Did you park in the driveway of the place you burglarized, in front of the residence, get dropped off, or park a distance away?

A. Seventy-two percent said that they parked a distance away, which is why you always want to call the police every time you see somebody in front of your condominium, townhouse, or residence who walks completely away from the area after parking. That's what I used to do when I just got started. This is why the police always check out cars parked in shopping mall lots after hours. Burglars think nothing of parking somewhere, and then walking a couple of miles or so, eventually working their way back to the car. If you ever see anybody park on the side of the street between your house and the next one, and walk down the street, call the police. When they arrive they will run the car license through the computer. If it's stolen or looks suspicious for any reason, they will put a stakeout team on it and wait for the culprit to get back and question him. Burglars are caught all the time like this. Twenty percent said that they got dropped off, which is the professional way of doing things. If you see anybody getting out of a vehicle and walk or run between residences, call the police at once. They don't mind coming to your area and checking these things. That's their job, and you'd feel a lot worse if you didn't call and somebody's house in the area got hit. Six percent said that they would park in the driveway of the house they were going to hit. These are the guys that plan on lugging off whatever they can. Again, if you see something that doesn't look right— call the police. Two percent said they would park in front of the place. I don't know why. Perhaps for a fast getaway.

What class of family did you come from?

A. Seventy-five percent said that they came from middle-class families, as did I. Second was lower-class, with 10 percent of the vote, while 6 percent said they were from upper-middle-class. Five percent claimed they came from very poor families. Four percent were from upper-class families.

Which class of family do burglars come from?. . . ALL CLASSES.

How much education did you have?

A. Sixty-two percent of the 300 inmates who took this survey said that they had quit school between grades eight and eleven. Eighteen percent said they either graduated from high school or completed some college. And 20 percent said they never made it past the seventh grade. I graduated from high school in 1965.

How many years did you spend doing burglaries?

A. Did you ever wonder how long a burglar can get away with continuous burglaries? The first bracket of six to ten years was chosen by 35 percent of the inmates. The second bracket of one to five years was next with 30 percent. Third was eleven to fifteen years with 25 percent and last was less than a year with 10 percent. How long can a burglar evade incarceration? I'd say anywhere from one day to fifteen years, or maybe longer. It's important to note that how long he's avoided the police is no real measure of a burglar's abilities.

How many burglaries do you feel that you have done in your lifetime?

A. Forty-six percent of the inmates said

they had done between 76-200 burglaries. Twenty-four percent visited 1-25 homes uninvited, while 19 percent admitted doing 501 or more. Remember this is per burglar. The remaining 11 percent said they had done 26-75 in their career as burglars . . . so far.

Do you use drugs or smoke "pot?"

A. A bull's-eye with 100 percent saying that they at least smoke pot, while 90 percent say they use Quaaludes, cocaine, etc. Not only was this a habit for them on the streets, but it hasn't changed any in prison, either in their usage of drugs or the ease of getting them. It's customary to walk on any prison compound and be able to buy about whatever you have the money for.

Would you be on drugs of any kind while doing the burglaries?

A. Here again it shows clearly that drugs are a major problem, with 94 percent saying that they would be at least on "pot" while doing burglaries, robberies and other crimes. They also said that if it weren't for the drugs they would never have entered a world of crime and come to prison. The other 6 percent stated that they were not on drugs while working, but used them immediately after the job was over. I had one inmate tell me that, when he'd be on cocaine, he would fear absolutely nothing and many times, as he called it, "went creeping" past people sitting in a chair in a home while they were reading the paper or watching TV facing the other way. He had to get money or jewelry for his next gram. He also said he carried a knife. I'll leave the addition to you.

Would your reason for doing burglaries be to either get money for drugs or items that you could sell to buy drugs?

A. Now we're getting to one of the roots of burglaries. I'm sure this information is well-known today and is no great discovery on my part. My survey shows that 70 percent answered yes to this question.

Would you steal drugs from a medicine cabinet?

A. Many people today are on medication, prescribed by doctors for a specific purpose, which, if taken in large enough quantities, will produce a high. I have never used drugs of any kind including "pot" and never took any drugs from medicine cabinets. However, 50 percent of the inmates said they have and do take drugs from cabinets, which they'd check out on every burglary. Forty percent said that they haven't ever looked in medicine cabinets for drugs. If I were to give my advice, I would say to ask your doctor if this is a drug (when prescribed) that people could use for an artificial high. If he says yes, store them in another place.

Would you ever check medicine cabinets for anything other than drugs?

A. Even though only 40 percent of the inmates said that they do check medicine cabinets for other things, like jewelry and money, I would recommend that nothing of any value be kept there. I myself once found a five-carat diamond behind a pill bottle. Sixty percent said that they wouldn't go to the medicine cabinet specifically for anything other than drugs.

How many of your friends do burglaries?

A. This question gives you just an idea of how many burglars there are out there today. Sixty percent of the inmates said that between one and five of their friends did burglaries. Thirty percent said six to ten of their friends were burglars. Six percent had eleven to fifteen friends also doing burglaries, and 4 percent told me that all of their friends were burglars. I wonder how many friends those 4 percent have? Every single person reading this book knows or has talked to a burglar, whether you know it or not.

If you had children, did they ever go with you while you were committing burglaries or any other crimes?

A. Twenty-five percent of the inmates with kids took them on burglaries. When asked "why" or what part they played, they said that the kids stayed in the car making it look as though a family were visiting at the house, and if caught, it would look more like it was just a simple mistake picking the wrong house. I was also told by an inmate that, when he makes drug deals, he plants the dope in his three-year-old son's jacket. The boy would be sitting beside him in the car so, if he got stopped and searched, they couldn't get him for possession. Burglaries and other crimes are being *taught* at a young age.

Have you ever burglarized a place more than once?

A. As you've read, one inmate told me that he hit one house nine times. And that was in a four-month period. In asking this question to the 300 inmates participating in the survey, 60 percent of them said that they hit the same house or business more than once. I myself have on several occasions for one reason or another hit the same residence more than once. In other words, if you burglarize a place one time and there's money lying all over the place and you score well, what do you have to lose in trying again? If your house has been burglarized before and your losses were large, batten down the hatches because there's a good chance that you'll be hit again by the same burglars. If you buy a Ford one year and have the best luck ever with it, when it comes time for a new one, why not try the same make again. Only makes sense, doesn't it?

CHAPTER 2

DOORS, LOCKS, WINDOWS

Hopefully now you have some idea of what the enemy is like. With the exception of the extreme professional, most burglars are lazy. Your job is to convince them of three things:

1. They're going to have a really tough time getting in.
2. If they do get in, they'll probably be caught.
3. If they don't get caught, it may just be because they'll be dead or seriously injured before the police get there.

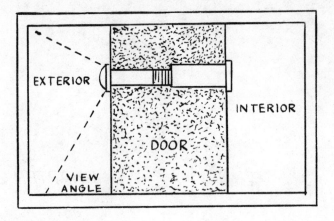

Door with Peephole.

The last two items will be treated in future chapters on alarm systems and mind deterrents. I don't want to underestimate the value of mind deterrents. That's what sets my Superthief concept of making a home safe apart from most crime-prevention programs, which always seem to emphasize hardware. Nonetheless, hardware can't be ignored.

There are many different kinds of doors on homes today and just as many in stores waiting their turn to be hung. For each different kind of door, there are as many different models of locks. Heavy-duty doors (those of hardwood and steel) are great, as are heavy-duty deadbolts. But as I've pointed out, neither heavy-duty doors nor heavy-duty locks offer any form of danger to a burglar. They simply slow him down. So, what does he care if he tears a door off with his tools? It doesn't bother him to steal your valuables. Why should it bother him to destroy your door, its casing, and your lock? No, doors and locks are not going to do it. Yes, they're good in preventing the kid walking through your yard, who at that moment decides he wants to break in but has no tools. But all real burglars today have tools, and some of them carry an entire hardware store with them. You can buy the best locks and doors and they're no competition at all against crowbars. Some pieces of hardware actually act as mind deterrents, in the sense that they may make a burglar think twice about hitting *your* home. If a particular door or lock makes him decide to go next door rather than through your door, he's been mentally deterred.

Doors

I hate to sound presumptuous, but most doors are a joke. They can be kicked in easily, or at least have a foot poked through them to make a hole that can be enlarged quickly. Forget about hollow doors. Forget about most wooden doors, unless they are solid and thick enough to resist an axe. Avoid doors with windows, unless they are very small and can be covered with a shade or curtains (you don't want people to be able to see into your house). And make sure the window is far enough from the lock so that the burglar can't reach through it and simply open the door. Forget about doors whose hinge pins are outside; a few taps and the door is off its hinges. The best doors are made of steel. And they should have a peephole device that provides at least a 180-degree view of what's going on outside.

Door Jambs

Door-jamb space is one of the biggest weaknesses

that any door and residence can provide a burglar. First, for those doors that do not have any form of secondary lock, it's commonly known that a knife, credit card or other thin object can easily and quickly open the door-knob lock if there is enough space between the door and its casing. This space is commonly found in hotels, motels, apartments and other rental properties. The doorjamb space in these places is almost always large enough to hide a small elephant. Solution: Have a second lock installed and, for the key-in-knob lock, install an anti-shim plate, which is a piece of metal attached to the door over the knob's side latch or bolt, preventing anything from being inserted. Remember though, that this device does not fill in the space all the way up to the door, so it only offers protection against the quicky burglar, with a credit card or knife. It will do nothing for the burglar who carries tools.

Locks

For years, Medeco was the only company that made pick-proof locks, and consequently had the only lock worth buying. A pick-proof lock literally is one that can't be opened by a locksmith—or burglar— using standard lock-picking tools or drills. There's a spring-loaded guard in the lock cylinder itself that prevents the insertion of anything in the keyhole other than a properly fitting key. So obviously you want a pick-proof lock, which many companies make today. Besides Medeco, Schlage and Fichet make good ones, and you want them to be casehardened (made of metal that has been treated to make it drill- and smash-resistant) as well, so they can't be drilled out in two minutes. One lock to

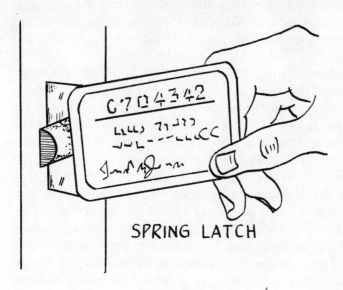

SPRING LATCH

Spring Latch Doorknob Lock.

Double-Sided Deadbolt Lock.

absolutely avoid is the spring-latch, key-in-knob type, which can be opened with nothing more than a credit card inserted between the bolt and door jamb.

Most people will tell you that you'll want double-sided deadbolts. A deadbolt literally is a lock whose bolt is dead, which is to say not activated by a spring. The bolt must be moved physically by the twisting of a key in the lock cylinder. In double-sided deadbolts, you have to use a key to open the door from the inside as well as the outside. In theory, on doors with windows, this will prevent a burglar from breaking the glass, reaching inside and opening the door. All the poor burglar can do—if he doesn't feel like tearing your door off its hinges—is break the window, and climb in through the hole. And, the theory goes, he's going to have a tough time lugging a TV through that little opening.

Maybe. But what if there's a fire, and you can't find the key and you get roasted in your own home? It defeats the purpose of the lock to leave the key in on the inside. Fire is a serious problem with these locks—so serious that in some places (like New York City) they're illegal for residential use. But there's another consideration.

Imagine you've got double-sided locks on all doors. A burglar has crawled through a window to gain entry and is still in the house as you return. You've trapped him in your home because he can't open any of the doors. You say he can just open a window and leave. Certain conditions *might* permit this. In my own case, once, the keys were left in a door lock on the inside, so I just opened it and left when I heard the car pull in. But will a burglar caught in this same predicament at your home be

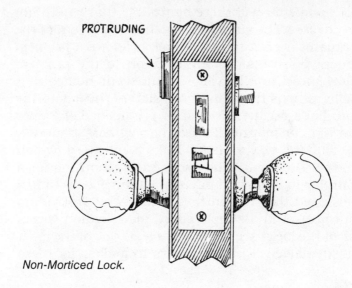

Non-Morticed Lock.

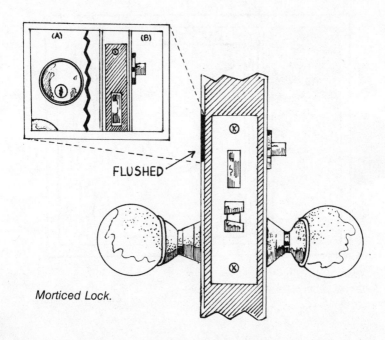

Morticed Lock.

so lucky? Or will there be trouble that you're not ready for? The survey shows that 95 percent of the inmates agreed that deadbolt locks are a problem once you're inside. The solution to the problem may mean annihilating an innocent homeowner who returns home in possession of the key to the burglar's escape. Even if you've opened the door for him, he may not like leaving a witness around...

The best way to install locks is morticed, which means flush with the door, leaving nothing for a burglar to grab with pliers or channel locks (a tool designed to grip and hold steady any protruding surface). And a simple guard plate, which covers all of the lock except the keyhole, is one of the most inexpensive yet valuable ways to make a lock less

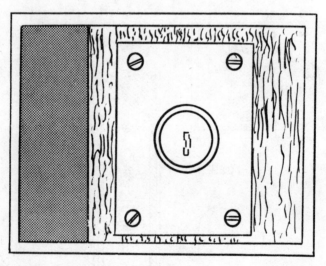

Guard Plate Protecting Lock Cylinder. (Mount plate with jimmy-proof screws.)

vulnerable. At the very least you should have a case-hardened collar.

No matter how good a lock is, most burglars today can still open your door—or at least destroy it. A screwdriver, a crowbar and channel locks are the only things necessary. There isn't any lock or door made that can continually fight battles against these tools. I remember attending a seminar put on by lock companies for the locksmiths in our area. They had samples of all the new locks out at that time, mostly deadbolts. They were set up in doors, and we were given tools to try and pull them off the door, fighting against case-hardened rings that cover lock cylinders, one-way screws and everything else that makes a deadbolt hard to pull off a door. And you know what? We couldn't get some of them off. They worked! They were almost impossible to take off the doors. But guess what? That's not the only problem with locks and doors. Pulling them off the door to gain entry is not the only way that burglars get past deadbolt locks. The problem is that a four-foot crowbar is capable of pulling open any door once it's wedged in the door jamb and wiggled back and forth a few times. The locks *are doing* what the manufacturers and locksmiths say they will, but that's only taking care of a very small part of the problem. It's like being thrown in a pool of alligators and sharks and having somebody shoot the alligators. You are still going to be eaten by the sharks.

So you ask what more can the lock companies do? I'll be perfectly honest with you. I don't know. They're doing the best they can to give us the best locks that money can buy. I am still 100 percent convinced that the only way to completely stop bur-

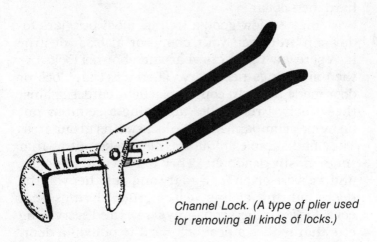

Channel Lock. (A type of plier used for removing all kinds of locks.)

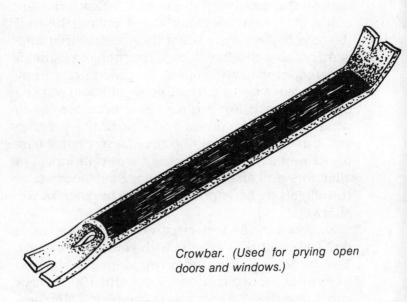

Crowbar. (Used for prying open doors and windows.)

glars is to make their mind want to go elsewhere: mind deterrents.

Sliding Glass Doors

I don't know about all parts of the country, but in Florida there are hundreds of thousands of homes with sliding glass doors. I'm sure that every other state also has homes with similar doors. Sixty percent of the inmates surveyed said that sliding glass doors are easier to break into than regular doors. That's because it's hard to secure them properly. Most people are lazy! They don't want to fool with the pin at the top because it's hard to move, and they don't want to mess with the bar that fits in the track to prevent the door from opening because Joey was using the bar for a baseball bat yesterday and he didn't bring it in.

There are some very effective locks made for sliding glass doors that will hold up against most tools—except the four-foot crowbar. Eighty-four percent of the inmates said a bar mounted to the door frame to jam the sliding doors makes them hard to get into. There are companies manufacturing bars for sliding glass doors that work at almost any angle. The best place to put a bar is in the middle, wedged halfway down between the sliding door and the wall. You can make one yourself out of a piece of dowel or anything else that's long enough. Or you can purchase one from a locksmith shop.

In the survey, the second choice for locks that made sliding glass doors difficult to open was the pin that slides through both doors at the top, preventing them from opening. Fourteen percent chose this security method, although I feel that any crowbar or other pry tool will easily force apart the two doors.

Steel Pin That is Inserted Through Both Sliding Glass Doors to Prevent Their Being Pried Open.

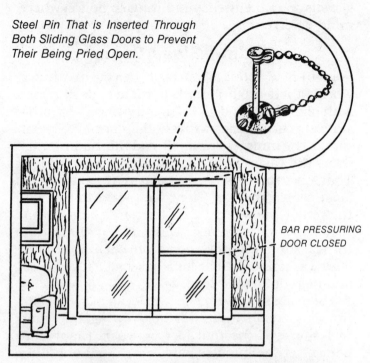

BAR PRESSURING DOOR CLOSED

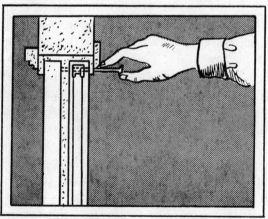

Another Way to Secure Sliding Glass Doors: Insert nails through both the track and the glass frame.

If you're worried about burglars breaking the glass, stand outside and look around. Could a burglar risk the noise of breaking one in your area? If so, then it's your choice. Do you want to overpower him with locks and give him no choice but to break it, or do you want to make it easy and possibly save your glass? I would place a bar in the middle as I've suggested and an alarm sticker on the outside. That's about all you can do.

The other 2 percent of the inmates said that the lock that comes on the sliding glass door itself gave them some problems. Luckily they never heard of screwdrivers and crowbars.

Chains and Doorknobs

For your protection while you are home, there are two items that I strongly recommend, especially for people living alone, women and the elderly. One of these items is an inside door chain. It offers no protection against tools. But if someone were to persuade you to open your door, and you still had the chain latched, and you noticed that he was up to no good, at least the chain would offer some resistance. In most cases this would scare a burglar off if a loud scream hit his ears. The best chains are those that have a small battery alarm attached so that when the door is opened to a certain degree the alarm will sound. There's NOTHING in the world an intruder can do to silence it from outside. He has to be on the inside to shut it off. They're cheap and very effective and really a must to have on your door while sleeping, if you don't have a house alarm. I can't say enough about how this item can save lives and prevent burglaries.

The other item is similar, a doorknob alarm. It hangs on the inside doorknob, and the instant the

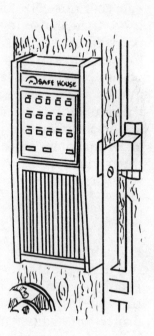

Door Alarm Mounted on Inside of Door. Once set, (you use a 3-digit code to set or shut-off) it sounds an alarm when door is opened.

Doorknob Alarm. It hooks over the inside doorknob and sounds an alarm when door is tampered with.

doorknob is touched (and I mean the slightest touch) on the outside, the alarm on the inside sounds and remains on for as long as a human hand is touching it. After the person lets go, it resets itself in about a minute.

Remember that both these alarms are only effective as a way of warning someone inside the house that an intruder is trying to gain entry. They offer no great protection when you're not home.

Windows

Most homes in areas where winter temperatures go below freezing have double hung windows: the ones where you open the window by sliding up the bottom half to cover the top half. These windows are a cinch to open with any kind of screwdriver or crowbar, or any other type of pry tool. The best and most effective and least expensive defensive action that a home owner can take with these windows is the old-fashioned trick of placing a small piece of plywood or dowel from the top half of the bottom window to the top of the window casing. This will offer the most resistance possible, and is about the only way of really securing these windows. Even though you've taken this measure to secure the double hung window, don't think that you can leave a million dollars on the counter. It's only going to stop the no-tool, impulsive burglar who just decides he wants a quick buck.

Florida is famous for jalousie windows. And since Florida was where my survey was taken, 76 percent of the inmates picked the jalousie window as the easiest to get into. There are all kinds of little tricks you can do to these windows, which are layered in separate sections that are cranked open. A lot of people try to glue them in place. The only thing that is effective is an alarm sticker along with the mind deterrents I'll explain later. Notice I haven't mentioned grills and bars over the glass. They're good for their purpose, but they're only going to make the burglar challenge the door itself instead of the glass. When I bought my first house in Florida, it had jalousie windows throughout. They were all changed within a month to awning windows, which just happened to be the survey's third choice as the best kind of window a home-owner can have. The second easiest to get into, with 16 percent of the vote, was the regular double hung window.

A Superthief Safe House

If I were building a house, I'd use regular cement blocks with a row of smaller blocks on the outside. I'd put one-inch-thick sheets of four-by-eight-foot plywood on the inside. (I don't want to tell you how many burglars have found it easier to go through walls than open doors!) All windows would have bullet-proof or wire-mesh glass. All doors would be steel, with no glass in them. The doors would have reverse hinges, so that the pins wouldn't be acces-sible. And they would open in. If a door opens in, it's easier to kick in, but can't be easily pried open with a crowbar. And it's unlikely that someone will find a log to batter a door down, or risk making the noise that battering generates.

I'd use Medeco locks on my doors. All Medeco locks are pick-proof, which means even a lock-smith can't open them. There are other good locks on the market. I would say Schlage is number two. Just make sure that any lock you buy is pick-proof,

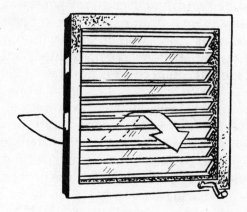

Jalousie Window.

Awning Window.

and case-hardened. And I wouldn't use double-sided deadbolts.

I'd have Rolladen shutters over all my windows. Once they're rolled down, they're almost too noisy or messy to fool with. And I wouldn't use window-unit air conditioners. They're very easy to knock out with one swift kick. If you need air conditioning, go central.

I'd have a standard closed-loop alarm system. In this system a series of wires extends through your house to different sensing devices connected to windows, doors, and perhaps pressure pads under rugs. If the devices are set off, the circuit is broken and it triggers the alarm. It's important to have all your windows protected with aluminum foil strips—the strips of tape you've seen in jewelry store windows. If the window is broken, the tape breaks the circuit and triggers the alarm. The installation of the foil must be done professionally. A real burglar can tell if you've done the wiring yourself. Window foil pays a double dividend: protecting your windows and acting as a great mind deterrent. I'd say it's the second thing to add to a house—after an alarm decal—whether or not it is actually connected to a system. My windows would also have magnetic breaker switches (see p. 56) and vibration suction cups. And I'd have plenty of pressure-sensitive mats under the carpeting. The alarm would be connected to police over a leased line (which is described in Chapter 3). And I'd have plenty of signs around announcing just that.

All window screens would be wired into the system, and the on/off switch would be inside, utilizing a digital pad (see p. 57). I'd have lights outside—high enough to make it impossible for a burglar to climb up and unscrew them.

*Windows Wired with Aluminum Foil
Tape.*

HINGE

*Bar Pressuring Sliding Glass Door
Closed.*

The main thing to remember here is the combination of deterrents. You want your house to announce quite clearly to a potential burglar that he's going to have a rough time getting in undetected, and if he does he's going to regret it.

And now, back to the inmates on the compound:

Which would you go through more often, doors or windows?

A. Naturally all burglars have gone through both in their days, but the question asks which they went through most. Seventy percent stated that they went through more windows than doors. The other 30 percent were like me—going in on their own two feet through the door. This shows a great weakness in windows and their locking mechanisms. It also shows how important window alarm stickers are.

Would you rather get in through a sliding glass door or a regular door, meaning which one offers less trouble?

A. Sixty percent said that sliding glass doors are easier to open than the regular type. I agree, but only because, with the glass on a sliding door, a burglar can see what he is up against and what he is accomplishing while working, whereas regular doors for the most part have stronger locks and offer no visual aid.

Did you ever pick locks?

A. First of all, let me explain to you, as I did to the inmates who took the survey, that picking locks requires tools that are sold only to locksmiths. Of course, if the tools can get into the hands of a locksmith, they can get into anybody's hands. Picking locks takes lots of practice and skill. Even a master locksmith can't pick open certain locks. Picking locks is not sliding a credit card or knife in the door jamb and pushing back the bolt. That's called answering an invitation. You're asking a burglar in if you leave that space wide open.

The survey shows that only 20 percent have picked or tried to pick locks (before their visit to prison), while the other 80 percent said they didn't pick locks. Even though I was a locksmith myself and had the proper tools, I didn't waste my time picking door locks when there were so many faster ways into a house. Don't worry about lock pickers: they are rare and there aren't that many good ones around anyway.

CHAPTER 3

ALARM SYSTEMS AND THE AIR HORN

With today's growing crime rate, alarm systems are appearing everywhere. They are being installed on everything from fire hydrants to outhouses, to prevent either use or theft of whatever they are protecting. There are hundreds of different companies producing them and hundreds more installing them.

Then there are, what I call, the "little boxes," which are sold through magazines and stores of all kinds. Little boxes are just that...small boxlike alarms that plug into the wall in your living room or whatever room you're trying to protect (a few

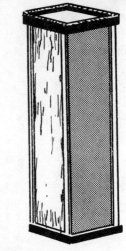

EXAMPLES OF THE "LITTLE BOXES."

A   *Ultrasonic Motion Detector. (Approximately 12 inches high.) When it senses motion in a room, it sends a signal to a "central processor" which sounds an alarm.*

B   *Central Processor. (Approximately 5 inches high by 11 inches wide.) Responds to signal from the motion detector and sounds a built-in alarm.*

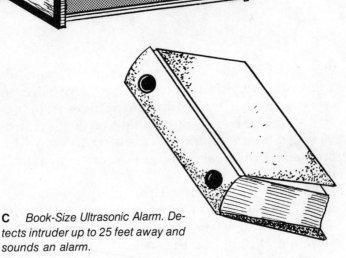

C   *Book-Size Ultrasonic Alarm. Detects intruder up to 25 feet away and sounds an alarm.*

claim to protect more than just one room). Some detect motion while others detect sound. All of these seem to have high-tech names. And they have their good and bad points.

The good points are that they will detect motion and they will detect sound—occasionally when there is neither one nor the other. They come with a built-in speaker for in-the-house alert only, but for a few dollars more you can add an outside speaker that will send sounds all over your neighborhood. Their cost is anywhere from $99 to $500. So much for the good points.

The bad points are that, unless you have installed the outside speaker, the alerting sounds are contained inside the home. Once inside all the burglar has to do is walk over to it—simple to find, since it's screaming, "Here I am!"—and unplug it. If the backup battery continues to keep it singing, he can place it under a couch cushion or smash it or carry it to the nearby sink. Five seconds of drinking water and it shuts off...forever. I used to collect them for bookends. Once, one of them had an outside speaker and, while shutting it off, I disconnected the speaker wires on the back of the alarm box and connected them to a nearby stereo. When I left I turned on the stereo for the neighborhood. I never did find out how they liked my choice of music.

There are some other problems with these little boxes. Some detect motion, and are constantly being set off by pets, or pictures falling off walls. And motion detectors generally work on a specific frequency, which means that stray transmissions or harmonics could trigger them. The sound detectors merely detect sound, and can't differentiate—as some of the ads claim they can—between

normal sounds and the sound of a burglary. Another variety is triggered by heat—for example, a
98-degree body entering a 45-degree basement.

None of these alarms—sound-, motion- or heat-
activated—are any good on their own, since they
are too easily deactivated. They may be useful as
part of a larger system.

Good residential and business alarms basically
operate and are installed in the same way. There
is a main panel, with lights, knobs and buttons all

Outside Alarm Speaker.

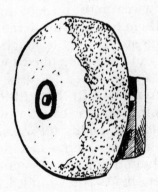

Inside "Reporter" Alarm.

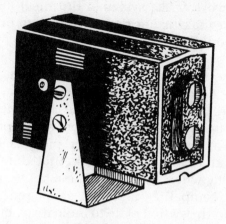

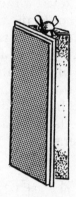

INFRARED BEAM ALARM
SYSTEM.

A   *Receiver Transmitter Unit.*
*Shoots a beam of invisible infrared
light across a space of up to 50 feet
to the Beam Reflector which bounces
light back. When beam is inter-
rupted, alarm is triggered.*

B   *Beam Reflector.*

over it, and wires—sometimes miles of wires
strung all through the walls and ceilings of the
home or business. The wires lead to sensing devices, which come in dozens of different kinds,
sizes and shapes. These range from pressure-sensitive mats under rugs, to foil tape on the windows,
from vibration suction cups on glass, to tiny wires
running through window screening, from motion
detectors, electric eyes, infrared beams and many
others, to the most common, the magnets on doors
and windows. Whenever these sensor devices are
disturbed and the circuit is broken, the main panel
gets the message and sends another message to
the alarm bell or siren to start singing.

These are worthwhile systems. But most alarm companies are making one drastic mistake: they're putting the on/off switch on the outside of the house, near or on the main door. Granted, they require a key, but that was no problem for me. Pick-proof, drill-proof, U.L.-listed alarm locks were all turned off in seconds, most of the time with no damage whatsoever. Even the type with round keys, which many people consider pick-proof, I could pick and leave undamaged so that they operated normally when the owner came home.

The alarm companies also put small red and white lights on the switch plate to indicate whether the system is on or off. Red is on and white is off. I had a little saying, "Red to white, you're all right." Alarm companies should be installing the switches inside the home, with a delay so that you can get

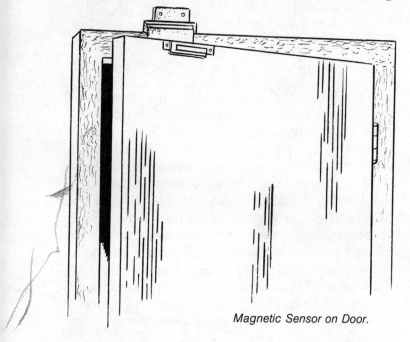

Magnetic Sensor on Door.

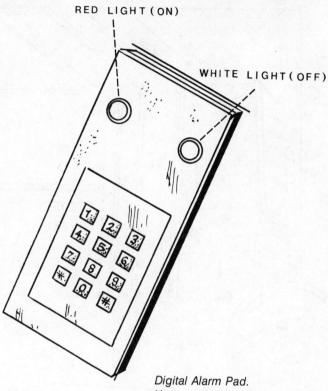

RED LIGHT (ON)

WHITE LIGHT (OFF)

Digital Alarm Pad.
You punch in code number to turn
system on or off.

in and out yourself without setting the alarm off. Be sure to have the alarm company install a digital telephone-type alarm pad that simply requires you to punch in a code number to turn it on or off. There are no keys to lose or worry about, just a simple code of between two and five numbers to memorize. Then your system will not be able to be beaten, unless someone comes through the roof or walls, which is rare in homes but common in businesses. If someone does enter without setting off an alarm, motion detectors, electric eyes and mats

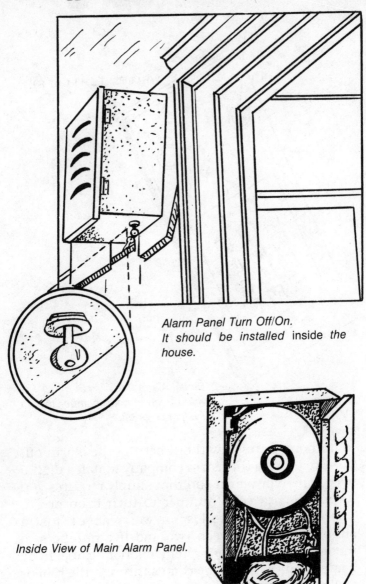

Alarm Panel Turn Off/On.
It should be installed inside the house.

Inside View of Main Alarm Panel.

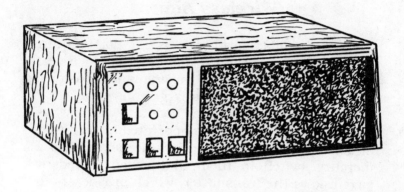

*Another of the "Little Boxes."
Detects motion within an area 50
feet long.*

under rugs all can catch anybody moving around inside. But these are useless in homes with pets.

If you have an existing alarm system which is operated by a key of any kind—either from the outside or inside—*replace it.* Call your alarm company and have them install a digital on/off pad instead. And don't pass your code out to just anybody.

Wireless Alarms

There are similar alarm systems that don't require wiring. These are called—appropriately—wireless systems and they stopped me on many occasions.

Wireless systems have a large control box that also acts as a receiver. Each door and window has a little plastic box, a battery-operated transmitter, attached to it. Usually these little boxes have a mercury switch in them that, when moved or jarred, keys the transmitter, which broadcasts to the main box and sets off the alarm.

Wired window screens and pressure-sensitive mats and any other types of sensors can be utilized with these wireless systems. At one time, I didn't know enough about them, and wanted to learn more. I knew there was no shut off done from the outside. It was a delayed system, in which you always had to walk through the same door when coming and going in order to delay the triggering of the alarm. When entering through this door, you tripped the alarm but had a predetermined amount of time to get in and shut the system off before it set off the bell and perhaps summoned the police. Opening any other door or window instantly sets off the alarm.

One of these systems is advertised in a TV commercial that depicts a little internal speaker in the main panel. When the alarm system has been tripped, it emits a high pitched squeal inside the house, letting anyone inside the house know that the alarm has been set off. This is a big mistake

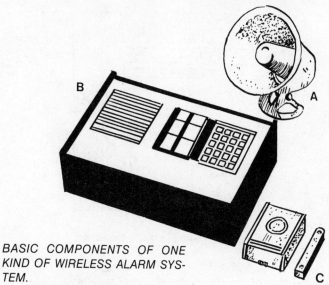

BASIC COMPONENTS OF ONE
KIND OF WIRELESS ALARM SYS-
TEM.
A   Outside Alarm Horn.
B   Central Signal Processor with
Built in Alarm.
Has built-in alarm which sounds
whenever wireless radio signal is
sent by a transmitter mounted on
door or window.
C   Transmitter and Magnet.
They are intended to be mounted on
doors and windows.

in design, though, because it instantly indicates
where the main alarm panel is. And since the system uses a transmitter, it might be easy to build
a jamming device.

Quite simply, if a person knew which door was
used to enter the house that tripped the alarm but
didn't set it off, he could break in that door, walk

Transmitter and Magnet Installed on Door.
When door is opened the separation of the transmitter and the magnet triggers a wireless radio signal which activates alarm in the "central signal processor."

into the house, listen for the high pitch squeal and walk right to it. When he got to it there were numerous things he could do: cut all the wires coming from the top of the box; pull the entire panel off its sliding rack; smash the unit a few times with a hammer, or throw water in one of the panel's many openings.

But how would you know which door had the delay? Common sense would tell you it was the door closest to the cars.

So I thought about it, and thought about it and would have bet a thousand dollars that I had the wireless system beat. One night I had to prove my theory was right. I went into an area that I had worked before, where I knew there was a house with a wireless alarm in it. I had passed it up once before. It was a Saturday night, and I knew these people always went out then. All I had to do was wait for them to leave and then I'd know which door had the delay. Once they were down the street, I started working on the door. Within three minutes I was ready to walk in. And sure enough, the sound I had heard on the TV commercial led me right to the alarm box. With a pair of wirecutters I snipped about six lines coming from the top of the box. The entire system was dead. Just from watching the TV commercial, I was able to beat the system. Thinking I would perfect my knowledge, I slid the alarm panel off its wall-mounted rack and took it with me. Then I went to a window and took a little plastic transmitter so I would have a complete system.

Before leaving, I checked for jewelry, but didn't find any more than a thousand dollars' worth. Figuring it wasn't even worth messing with, I left it lying on the kitchen table. With my portable radio, I called my driver and told her to meet me a block from where she had dropped me off. I put the alarm in the trunk and called it a night. I would love to have heard their call to the police that night: "I don't understand. They left my good jewelry on the kitchen table and stole my alarm system!"

At home in the weeks to come, I worked and played with the system, learning it so well that I could walk up to any wireless alarm system and make fools of the company.

In the nights to follow I did just that. Sometimes I would take the panel off the wall and leave it in front of the door outside so the owners wouldn't have too far to go to shut it off!

Silent Alarms

Many people think that silent alarms—which don't ring bells, but just summon the police—are just what the doctor ordered. That could be, but it would have to be a doctor of psychiatry. Silent alarms are good for banks and stores if you are not the owner, but for residences they are very dangerous. First of all, when an undesirable is attempting to break into your residence, you should want your alarm system to detect him and *scare him off* with loud noise as soon as possible. If the alarm is silent and he's the nervous type, he's going to break in, trip the alarm (which will make no noise at the home), giving him time to run in and have at least five minutes before the police are even in the area. Do you realize what a burglar who is in a hurry can grab in five minutes? He could clean the place out.

The major point here is that you want to scare the burglar. If he's strong-headed enough to want to break into a house with an alarm system, you at least want him to know that the thing is working. You want all that noise! That way he'll assume that the police are coming. Yes, he may linger a few minutes to grab a couple of obvious items. But it's more likely that he's going to get the hell out of there. And in virtually every case, he's not going to stick around long enough to create an O.K. Corral.

A silent alarm generally works by using a phone dialer, which calls an alarm company, which in turn calls the police. There is a delay of between five and fifteen minutes before the police can get there. That's plenty of time for a burglar to clean your house out, or at least take a few things that you will miss. But let's say that the police just happen to be in the area, and that they move in in time to trap him in the residence. They have him cornered. The place is surrounded, just like on TV...and you've heard of those people who swear they won't be taken alive, haven't you? Well, O.K. Corral, here we come! Shoot-out city! The problem here is that your house or business is eating the bullets. Have you ever seen a house that has been fed two million bullets, five tear gas canisters, six small grenades and a pear tree? Well, neither have I, but it's only common sense that it's not going to be as pretty as when you left. In other words, not only is a silent alarm a joke because it might not do its job, but if it does its job, that means you're using your home as rat bait, to catch some burglar who is probably the kid down the street anyway. Now if you want to risk your house to catch a burglar, then silent alarms are for you. The same situation could have happened with somebody asleep at home and then there really would have been some problem. I do not recommend silent alarms for residential use. Stores, banks and businesses may warrant them.

Personal Body Alarms

In the last ten years stores everywhere have been equipped with every type of alarm imaginable. One of the most unique of all was the cash register alarm: when the last bill was pulled out, the weighted arm holding the money down closed a circuit, keying a silent alarm to inform the police of a robbery in progress. Eventually the word got around, and it was for the most part discontinued.

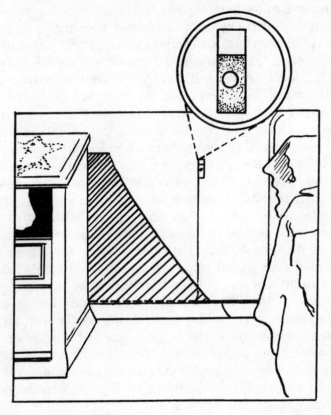

Panic Alarm Button Mounted Next
to Bed.

Most stores went to a system used in banks, with
a button under the counter or on the floor. When
this "panic button" was pressed, it set off a silent
alarm that summoned the police. The only problem
was if the cashier was in an aisle putting away

stock (as is done in small convenience stores) and a couple entered the store to rob the register, the clerk couldn't get to this button in time. So then something else had to be done, something with which the store operator, wherever he was in the store, could activate the alarm. It wasn't long before a very small device was invented that transmitted to a receiver in the backroom of the store, which in turn summoned the police. It was small enough so that the clerk could carry it on his person and know that all he had to do was press the button and help would be en route. Some of these systems use telephone lines, while others actually have small transmitters at the store that can transmit on police frequencies, allowing all of the patrol cars on that channel to hear the robbery in progress on their radios.

Effective isn't the word, for this idea has helped catch hundreds of robbers. Such a great thing, manufacturers thought, that they came out with a residential version of this incredible little device. Today, senior citizens, sick people, and wheelchair users alike can wear this small device around the neck and know that with the mere touch of a button, the police will be en route.

I saw an ad recently that touted this service for the residence. The ad pointed out some of the uses that I've named above, and also mentioned several others that I feel should get careful thought before utilization.

Let me set up a very possible hypothetical incident. Let's say that you're a wheelchair user, home alone (which many are) or that you're a senior citizen and not quite as spunky as in your earlier days. While at home you hear somebody breaking in. And let's say you have this little transmitter hanging around your neck and all you have to do is press the button and the police will be en route to your house. OK, so here you are, more or less helpless for one reason or another. A burglar or robber is breaking in, you've pressed the button and the police are on the way. Does the burglar know this? How could he? There's no way! Is he going to stop breaking in? Why should he? As far as he knows there's no trouble yet. No bell or siren has gone off. So on with his breaking in he goes until he finally gets in. Now he's in, confronts you (and if you're elderly or in a wheelchair, then he's definitely going to) and in the process of his gathering up what he came for, the police arrive and do what they've been trained to do...surround the place. Assume the police are smart and don't start yelling for him to come out (even though this could happen, putting you in very serious trouble), but as the intruder starts out, he sees one of their cars or even one of the police. You don't think he's going to continue out, do you? There is a chance that the person inside with him would make a pretty good hostage, isn't there? Add up what could happen from here. You might think this situation I just made up is one in a million. But if you were to visit your police station and check through their records, you'd soon see I have a very important point here. Hostage situations are common.

The Air Horn

I've said that silent alarms are dangerous, and that it's foolish to summon the police using a phone line unless you've made sure, by creating enough noise to awaken the dead, that the burglar knows the police will come. But what if the burglar thinks he can take care of the noise? And what if he thinks he can prevent the police from being notified by cutting your phone line? And, having done all this, what if he breaks into your house when you're inside?

If you walk outside your house, you'll find where the phone line gets in through the wall, and see just how easy it is to cut off your main connection with the world (ham operators and C.B. nuts are excluded).

In the survey, 63 percent of the inmates said that they cut phone lines. Now naturally this is not at every house they burglarize. But the fact still remains, they have cut phone lines in their past burglaries.

How to protect ourselves in case this should happen while we're at home is something that should be looked into very seriously. I'm going to be painting several pictures here, to show you the effect of my idea as it was presented to the inmates. Picture these things happening to you or your children, parents, neighbors, friends or other relatives. If you checked with your police department you would see that they happen more than you would imagine. Remember that this whole issue revolves around the telephone.

As I said in the opening lines of this book, you're home alone...you see a stranger...you hear noises...you reach for the phone...

...AND IT'S DEAD!

What to do now?

Or remember the hostage situations referred to in discussing personal body alarms.

What to do in that situation?

Oh, some of you will grab that gun by the bedside table and either blow out his brains or yours. But before you do that, did you ever think it could be the kid two houses down, who is drunk and thinks this is his own house—and his mother has locked him out. Can't happen? You better believe it can. I remember one night in New Hampshire at my place in the mountains, on a weekend when my parents had come to visit for a few days. I was awakened at about 2:30 by a noise in the living room. I got out of bed and walked down the hall to find a naked man sitting in one of my living room chairs with his clothes piled on the floor. He was drunk out of his mind and had no idea where he was. Up there, then, you didn't have to lock the doors (until that night), so he just walked in. Soon everybody was up and the police were on the scene. But the point is, that gun in your hands could shoot the wrong person—and you will either go to prison or pay mentally for the rest of your life. If you don't think this could happen to you, because you're too alert, then what about your parents, or kids, or somebody else you care about? The fact is—police reports will prove what I'm saying—this does happen every day of the week, several times over, in every state in the U.S.

The picture again is that you're home, hear somebody breaking in, run to your phone and it's dead. You fear going out, don't have guns or don't want to shoot anybody if you do. What do you do?

The answer is compound: scare the devil out of whoever is breaking in; alert *all* of the neighbors that something is wrong; send the intruder running like hell, knowing that he'd better not ever come back to this place again; and get one or more of your neighbors to call the police.

How to do all this from inside of your home? What could do it? An alarm, you say? Yes, that would do it. But most people do not have alarms. You do want to alarm the people and scare the burglar off, but that is alarming them...not an alarm. Don't know? Well it's something that's been on the market now for years. That's right. It's an existing product, so if you're thinking it's something I've invented to make millions, you're wrong. That would be nice, but that's not the case.

I am talking about an "air horn," the kind small boat owners use on their boats. It's nothing more than a can of pressurized freon with about a five-inch horn attached. These horns can be heard for one mile over water.

So what do you do with it, you ask? You go to a window on the opposite side of your residence from where you hear the intruder breaking in and open it just enough so that the horn's mouth can aim its words out the window. And then you squeeze, and squeeze, and I'm telling you right now, anybody...whether they're drunks, burglars, Peeping Toms, prowlers, trespassers or anything living, including dogs...is going to be hot-footing it as fast as they can.

First of all, anyone who thought there was nobody home is now in a state of shock, and isn't mentally prepared to deal with a burglary. The ones who did know somebody was home, but thought they had cured all problems by cutting the phone line, have just bitten their tongues. So they're going to be gone in seconds, too.

When you buy your horn, you should discuss it with your neighbors, so they will know what to do should they ever hear it screaming into the night or day. You might also advise them to purchase one of these life-saving, crime-stopping devices for their own protection. The more residents that have them the better the chances of catching the culprits. What am I basing that on? Seventy-two percent of the inmates said that when doing their crimes they parked a distance away and walked to wherever it was they were heading. That means that, like myself, they are walking around neighborhoods, in between houses, over fences and anywhere else they feel like going, *all on foot.* Now if they're in your yard and you see them peeking in, you have two choices. One, walk to the window and let them see you, hoping that you scare them away, then call the police...if you can. Or second, you can go to an opposite side window and blast your horn, alerting everybody within at least a quarter of a mile that there is either a prowler or burglar in the area. Then look out your windows and turn on your lights. This way you can—if you see him running—give the police sufficient information to track him down. Remember, his car is down the street and he's got to get to it. If everybody is out and about, lights on, etc., he's going to panic and run right into trouble someplace soon.

But most importantly, you've scared him away from your home and property, and could have saved your life. Now let's say that this situation has happened someplace, but the guy gets away. I myself *might* have worked that area one more time if it wasn't too close a call, but if it happened again and I got away, you'd better believe that I never would have worked that area again. It wouldn't be long before word about these horns spread throughout the community of burglars and other undesirables. Wouldn't it be nice if there were signs on roadsides similar to crime-watch signs, with a picture of a horn and under it a warning:

"Horn-Protected Neighborhoods." Something to give them the advanced NOTIFICATION to think "Oh, no, it's another one of those areas." Sound like a crazy idea? Tell me this: If somebody had approached you about six months before the hula hoop came out, and told you this was going to be a tremendous fad and everyone was going to be buying one, what would you have said then? Have you ever heard, "It takes money...to make money?" Sure you have. Well, here's a new one for you. "It takes people with open minds to get good ideas and programs off the ground." For the ridiculously low investment that this idea involves, and considering what it will do for your community and yourself, you've got absolutely nothing to lose by trying it.

One of my survey questions backs up my way of thinking:

If you had cut the phone lines of a resident you were burglarizing and at some point heard from inside that same residence, coming from the window, an extremely loud horn, what would you do?

Ready for this? One hundred percent stated that they'd be gone in a second, or something similar. I'd quote some of the exact answers, but I'd rather keep this book readable for all ages. It might be "my way of thinking," but it's also that of 300 inmates who took the survey. It doesn't matter how smart or dumb you are: a loud horn blasting away as loud as this horn is means trouble. And they all know it.

How much do they cost? They are anywhere from $10 to $15, but even if they were $20 it's the best thing you could ever buy for crime prevention and your safety. There is a smaller model for about

$5.95 and it will work, but it's much better suited for a personal protection device carried by women in their purse. Any boat supply store will either have them or will tell you where you can get one. The best brand is Falcon. When you get yours, show it to your neighbors and explain its usage and what it can do for them. The more people who have them and know of their purpose, the more effective the system becomes.

This horn can also be a lifesaver in connection with fires when used as a warning device by a person awakened by smoke, heat or flames.

Also remember that when you purchase your horn and bring it home, it is important to explain its operation and protection capabilities to family and neighbors. DO NOT MAKE IT SOUND. Remember that you're telling them that this sound means trouble of some kind and if you explain that and then go blasting it at every neighbor's house where you're showing it, the old "crying wolf" problem will soon set in. All you have to do is point out where you squeeze the trigger and they'll know how to activate it when and if needed. It is also *imperative* that all children be WARNED STRONGLY that this is not a play toy and should not be touched except in extreme emergencies. If you don't have that control, then keep the horn out of their sight and reach. It must never be played with and should be put away during parties—whether the parties are for children or adults. Once the horn is abused—by a curious child or a drunk adult—it will not only become worthless in your neighborhood, but in others as well. This can be a very effective crime deterrent, crime stopper and lifesaver if you and your crime-prevention program will adopt it with a *very positive attitude.*

The Problem with Today's Alarm Systems

I've told you a little bit about alarms, how they work, which systems are good and which ones are bad, and now I'm going to tell you the fault with all alarm systems today. They all detect intruders and that's really the problem right there in that one word, "intruders."

Intrude means to invade, to force in without permission, but in burglary it means plain and simple "BREAK IN." An intruder in the burglary business means a person who BREAKS INTO a place. When they do that and the place has an alarm, the alarm does its job and detects the intruder. At least that's what alarms are supposed to be for anyway, to detect a burglar. OK, let's leave this just for a moment and look at the cost of alarm systems today. For my two-bedroom house in Florida, I paid $4,500 for an alarm system in 1977. I could have paid as little as $1,500 but knowing a little bit about the business I had a good one installed. Today a system for an average house (which mine was) would be at least $2,200 and the sky is the limit on the top price. A mansion or even a $2–300,000 house today would cost at least $5,000, up to $20,000, for a good effective alarm. And it would be for that price, 90 percent unbeatable. I imagine in a $150,000 home that the doors are all solid hardwood, probably hand-engraved, with special locks and heavy duty door casings. Good alarm system inside and...What?...

What was the word I just used. Inside? Alarm system inside? Now let's see, the alarm system is inside, as are the sensing devices, and, as I mentioned earlier, the word intrude means BREAK IN. Now if the sensors are on the inside, but do not sense anything until they detect intrusion, that means that, in order for your alarm system to do anything for you, in order for it to start screaming, "Help, help," somebody has to smash that special glass window you ordered and waited a long time to get (and will again the second time—if they still make them at all). That means that the hardwood door that you had flown in from a foreign country and the expensive locks will have been more than likely destroyed or at least damaged before your alarm system wakes up.

Now stop for a minute and picture this. Imagine you own a $200,000 house. You know the alarm company is going to charge you anywhere from $5,000 to $20,000 for a good alarm system. And you know how you feel about your home, your belongings and that peace of mind you bought with your alarm. You feel you are really in the safety zone. But imagine a burglar standing at your front door, with a four-foot crowbar. He unscrews the light that would expose him to the neighbors across the street, and then he destroys your door, its two locks, the door casing and basically does $2,000 worth of damage (or even $500) trying to get it open. Believe me, he's going to get it open, and the alarm *is* going to go off instantly, with bells all over the place. But did he run in (even with the bells ringing) and grab a TV, or a jewelry box, or a lamp worth $5,000, or a picture on the wall worth a million before he ran off into the night? And even if he didn't... tell me, how are you going to feel about your alarm system that you spent so much money for? Do you think it did its job? Do you feel

as good about it as you did when the alarm company was pulling away from the house the day they
installed it? There's not an alarm system out there
(with the average installation) that detects a damn
thing until somebody has done X amount of damage, not to mention probably getting away with
something before it starts its bells ringing.

Is that your idea of an alarm? I guess it is; that's
what every alarm in every home, bank, store or
business is all about. Even I had one at my house.
You'll notice I said, "with the average installation."
That means that, for lots of extra dollars, you could
fill your yard with electric eyes, so that when somebody walked through one of them, it would set off
the alarm, before any damage was done to the
home. Sounds good, doesn't it? Except for a couple
of things. Every time dogs or cats enter your yard
and pass through one of these beams, off goes your
alarm. And if they are put up high enough so that
animals won't set them off, then they're high
enough for a person to crawl under, and if not,
someone can step over them. Besides this, electric
eyes are usually not used for this purpose. I never
ran into them set up for catching trespassers or
would-be burglars, but a few homes I did see had
them set up at the seawall in the backyard bor-
dering the Intracoastal Waterway, so that anybody
pulling a boat alongside the homeowner's dock and
getting out would trip the alarm as soon as they
entered the yard. But they are easily detected no
matter where they're set up and easier to beat. I've
beaten them on several dozen occasions.

While working on a place alone one night I noticed four adults leaving a beautiful house across
the street after turning their alarm on. I watched
them get into their Cadillac and drive down the

road. It was safer taking advantage of places when I had just seen the people leave, because I knew they would be gone awhile. So I picked up my bag and left the place I was, deciding this other place looked better. Heading across the street I entered their yard. At this time I had no idea of how to turn off alarms, so I had to pass on most houses with them. But not until I had checked them out closely, to see if the system could be beaten.

As I walked around the house, I came to a screened-in pool in the back. If you were to look at the house from the air, it would appear like the letter "C" with the pool in the middle. Opening the screen carefully, I listened for alarm bells, etc., but heard nothing. Once inside the screened-in patio, I noticed the entire back of the house was sliding glass doors. But I didn't see any alarm tape or any other type of detection devices on any of them. So I stood there a minute thinking and wondering why and finally figured that they must have used some other type of sensor. Flashlight in hand I looked around. There it was, about eighteen inches above the floor in the corner: an electric eye pointing across the "C"-shaped house, all the way to the other end of the house. If anything walked up to the back of the house, it would walk through the eye, which would set off the alarm. Now it was obvious why they didn't wire all the doors across the back. You couldn't get near them anyway.

At least, that's what I thought the system was like. I again stood still looking at the eyes. AH HA! I got it. I couldn't walk through it and it would be very dangerous jumping over it, but I could crawl under the beam, trying not to break it even for that one instant that would set it off. Should that happen, I had my police radio on anyway, in case it was a silent alarm. I would get the report the same time the cops did and be gone. So I lay down on the floor looking at the eye—hoping it didn't look at me.

It would be very close if I could make it. I slid my bag under first, and then I got down as flat as I could. I inched and inched very slowly all the way to the door. When I got there, I looked back at the eyes, winking at both of them before standing. Looking on the inside of the sliding glass door in the kitchen, I saw a small rug. I thought there could be a pressure-sensitive mat under it, so if I got that far I had to step over it. Carefully removing the international key—a crowbar—from my bag, I opened the door, hoping I was right about the door not being wired. It opened with no noise of alarms. I stepped over the rug after closing the doors behind me. I was now inside the kitchen with no alarms set off. I was standing by the refrigerator so I got a Pepsi. I looked for something to eat, and found one banana and two pears. I started to walk down a long hall that led along the inside of the house. On the side of the wall was an alarm switch that could be turned on or off if you had the key. The light was red. It was on. I still risked the chance of walking into another electric eye somewhere before I knew it. Slowly I walked all the way down to the master bedroom. There on the wall was another alarm shutoff, this time with the key in it. I tried it. The light went from red to white. I turned it back on, leaving it on in case the people came home. That way they wouldn't notice that it was off and call the police. And if they turned it off, I'd see it and know I had to get out of there fast. The bedroom was really cluttered with all kinds of things. They collected knickknacks and junk. I started looking for the lady of the house's jewelry, and found nothing. But there was a safe in the closet. My heart stopped as usual. Standing there, I took a sip of Pepsi and a bite from the banana and one from the pear. Then I called my driver in code, saying that I would be busy and making a lot of noise. She would have to be the ears and listen to the police radios for me in case I missed any of it. I would still be listening, but she would be double protection, and could reach me on my other two-way radio, if need be.

I tried the safe door, but it was locked. Before working on the safe, I walked to the sliding glass doors that were right behind me and unlocked them. I didn't open them, since I had left the alarm on. Then I checked the track to make sure there was not a piece of wood in it. There was, so I took it out. Now I had a quick exit if there was trouble. The alarm system protected me from its owners because they could not get in without the red light turning white, and as soon as it did, I would know they were home and could open the door that I had just unlocked.

So with that, I pulled the safe out of the closet where I would have more room to work. I flipped it up on its top and started pulling the bottom off. I got the wheel dolly off, then a piece of sheet metal, and then I had to beat through six inches of cement and another piece of sheet metal. About thirty minutes later I could get one hand in the hole I had made. I took two bites from my last pear, and started pulling stuff out. Little by little it emerged. A few of his cufflinks and some change and that's about it. I struggled to get my hand in the little hole and reached in trying to find anything else left, but found nothing. Where was it? This couldn't be it. I didn't have a hundred dollars yet. I went through the closet checking further, but found nothing. I looked on the top shelf and saw a lot of lady's wigs and more bags, etc. I went to a desk in the bedroom. Nothing but junk in it. I left the bedroom for a minute and went into the living room to judge the furniture. It was very expensive. Then I checked a few more rooms: also expensive furniture. I walked back into the bedroom and into the closet again. I stood up on a little stepladder, which told me they used it for putting things up on the shelf. I looked around and saw all kinds of bags. I never liked messing with all these bags. There was one there that looked as if it could have held a roll of toilet paper. It was used for hair rollers. At least that's what was on top. After taking a few out, I pulled the bag off the shelf. It fell out of my hands onto the floor. Damn thing weighed ten pounds!

I got down and picked it up. There were only a handful of hair rollers on top. Under them the bag was filled with gold and diamonds, all first-class stuff. I placed the whole little bag in my sack, and checked around to make sure I had left nothing. Still a bit thirsty I went to the kitchen and had a glass of orange juice. There was a big Hershey bar sitting on the counter. I opened it and ate what I wanted and then wrapped it up so it wouldn't get stale. Back in the bedroom I got the key to the alarm, turning it off at the same time. Then I walked down the hall for the last time and stood at the front door. After unlocking it, I left through that door, stopping at the alarm switch on the outside to turn it on again so the house would be protected against burglars. Then I left the key in the driveway, so they wouldn't have to have another one made. Reaching for my Motorola portable, I called my driver who picked me up a block down from the house.

There were a couple of good-sized diamonds in the package. The next day I called my fence and told him to bring about $45,000 with him. He did. He worked the package, weighing it out and counting all the diamonds. We made about $43,000 for all of it. I drove down to the local Chevy dealer looking for a new car that I had wanted for a long time. It was the first of the 1978 silver anniversary edition Corvettes that had come in, so I only had a few to choose from. A yellow one caught my eye. I went over to it and took it for a test ride. It was nice. I told the salesman, "I'll take it. Do what you have to do to it. I'll be back in an hour."

He said, "Impossible."

I said, "I'll bet you a hundred dollars it's not."

The rest of the money was spent on speeding tickets.

I tell you all this not to brag. The reality is that no home is invincible, even with detectors designed to keep burglars away from the house. But if you have an alarm system installed, don't be foolish enough to give a burglar a break. Always turn it on. And never leave a key in a panel!

There is one way I know of to keep burglars from breaking into your home, without using electric eyes—which you've already seen aren't foolproof. If you have a key switch installed in your door already, don't have the alarm company remove it when they come to install the inside digital key pad. Just ask them to wire the switch into the alarm's circuitry. That way, if any clever burglar tries to pick the system off, he'll set the alarm off. Having keyless digital pads will also take care of lost keys, or the key you never got back from the maid you fired. And while you're at it, have the alarm company replace the white bulb with a red one. This way they'll both be red. Only you will know whether right or left, top or bottom is the on position. It'll drive a burglar crazy. At least, it drove me crazy a few times.

Telephone Lines

Many burglars cut phone lines for one reason or another, usually thinking that they are disarming an alarm system if there is one. Or I should say disarming its telephone dialing capability—which summons help. Most alarm systems do have telephone dialers. But unless the owners of such residences or businesses have rented a "leased" or "balanced" line from the phone company, cutting the line *will* terminate the dialing capability.

A leased or balanced line is like an open circuit from the alarm to a monitoring post. Sometimes these monitoring posts are at the police station, but most commonly they are found at an alarm company's own monitoring station. If a phone line with a leased-line service as part of the alarm system is cut, it will instantly ring bells and send meter needles tumbling, both indicating that the phone line has been tampered with. It is a foolproof system to the degree that the chances of somebody beating it by cutting a line are one in a million. But, the leased line does cost anywhere from $25 to $40 a month per line. Banks, jewelry stores and coin shops almost always utilize a leased line.

Anyone who can't afford this monthly service but would still like to reap the benefits of a leased line...can't! But the very next best thing is to make any person who intends to cut your phone line think that it will automatically summon help even when cut. Now how can we accomplish this? Very simple. Mind games: mental deterrents. Just have a small sign made up (or make it up yourself) that states, "This house's telephone utilizes the 'leased line.' Any tampering with or cutting of these wires automatically sets off indicators at the monitoring station, which in turn sends the police." Again, this sign offers a danger to any undesirable who has in mind tampering with your phone line. Will it actually deter someone from messing with your phone line? One way of answering this is to say that it definitely won't if you don't use the idea. Another answer is every little bit helps. If enough mind deterrents are used, your home will offer too much danger to a potential burglar's well-being for him to continue. One thing for sure is that you've got nothing to lose.

Alarm Do's and Don't's

• Always tell your neighbors what to do if your alarm goes off. This may be as simple as phoning you at work, or calling the police.

• Never have an alarm system that shuts itself off. It may bother the neighbors, but that's one of the things it's supposed to do.

• Don't rely on a single bell or siren. They can be incapacitated by a .22-caliber gun with a silencer, pillows, foam, etc. Always hide at least one siren under the eaves of the house where it can't be easily reached.

• Beware of alarms that frequently set themselves

off, such as ones that use heat, noise or motion detectors, or electric eyes. Remember the story of the boy who cried wolf. Eventually the police may NOT come. A few burglars have told me that they'd set an alarm off until the police wouldn't come, and then just walk into the house. Some communities are establishing fines for false alarms. In some places in Florida now, the charge is $100.

As for the other inmates...

Would visual signs of an alarm system deter you?

A. Ninety-two percent of the 300 inmates who took the survey stated that it would deter them if they saw alarm tape on windows, wired screens, suction cups on the inside of windows (detecting vibration) or bells on the outside walls of a home. Eight percent said that it wouldn't faze them a bit. They'd try to shut it off and if they failed, run for it. As for myself, I wouldn't hit a house unless it had an alarm. They offered me challenges of all kinds and kept my mind on the edge of a cliff.

Have you ever passed on doing a burglary because, while you were standing at the door or window, you saw an alarm sticker

advising you that these premises had alarms?

A. Now we are in the realm of our mind games—the little clever, inexpensive ideas that set a burglar's mind to thinking, "Do they or don't they?" And then to coming to the conclusion, "Who knows but why take a chance?" Before I give you the percentages of the results of this question, let me give you the sample alarm sticker I presented to the burglars I questioned. I'd seen many alarm stickers in my past ventures that didn't impress me, so I came up with a new one. It's simple, and has the right words to mess up a burglar's mind to the point where he doesn't know what to do, so he leaves. Remember...mind games are the answer. The alarm sticker I asked the survey participants to respond to read:

MOTION DETECTOR ALARM

This Building is Equipped with
Laser-Type Motion Detector Devices.
Bodily Movement Inside will Set Off
Audible or Silent Alarm.

Eighty-five percent said that after reading such a notice they would leave and go elsewhere. Why take the chance? And then there's the 15 percent who said that they would try and, if there was an alarm, run for it. Alarm stickers are good, but better yet if they have unusual phrasing like the one I used in the question.

Did you ever bypass alarms?

A. Bypassing alarms is something that you've seen on *Mission Impossible.* It means that you don't shut the alarm off, but rather try and find a way to sneak past part of it. On *Mission Impossible* they often used alligator wire leads and ran them from one point to another, cutting out a certain area of the system. In my mind anybody who attempts a stunt like this IS attempting an impossible mission. I say this because what good is it to somehow bypass a door or window only to walk into the dwelling and step on a rug mat (pressure-sensitive device) or to trip a motion detector? I had a rule that I used in the latter part of my burglary career. If I couldn't shut the alarm system off completely—the hell with the place. The results of the survey showed that 55 percent said they had bypassed alarms, while 45 percent said they had not.

Did you ever turn off (NOT BYPASS) alarms?

A. This question shows strong results with 95 percent saying that they had not and could not turn alarms off. The 5 percent that said they had, in my estimation, only stumbled on a particular freak incident where the home owner left the keys in the alarm or they found an on/off light-type switch on the wall that turned off the alarm. When questioned if they ever picked (with picks) the alarm off or in other clever ways shut it off, 100 percent said no. There are a couple of messages here. Don't leave your keys in your alarm and don't use a switch that's in view of an intruder.

Do you ever cut phone lines?

A. The telephone is one of the most important things a person has in a place of residence. It is not only good for chitchat, but invaluable when used for calling the doctor, taxicab, repair man, fire department, police, ambulance, etc. Unfortunately, 63 percent of the burglars I surveyed said that they cut phone lines right at the side of your home, where the wires enter through the wall.

Would you ever shut off the electricity from outside the home at its main power box or a main switch located elsewhere, thinking it was also shutting off the alarm system?

A. Only 15 percent said that they had at one time or another shut the electricity off. It is a total waste of time because all alarm systems are backed up with their own battery.

CHAPTER 4

SUPERTHIEF'S M.D.*

By now you should have a good idea of what you're
up against in the way of burglars, and most of the
standard ways that traditional crime-prevention
programs try to stop them: doors, locks and alarm
systems. Imagine you're a burglar. It's 9:00 P.M.
You've checked out a target house, you think you've
found a vulnerable back door, and as you're reaching for your crowbar, you trip over something. You
pull out your flashlight to look down, and discover
a dog dish that's about two feet in diameter.

What are you going to do?

*Mental Deterrents

91

Well, I'll tell you what 99 percent of the burglars out there are going to do: they're going to run so fast that they won't ever get a chance to see what kind of gargantuan animal might eat out of a dish that size.

The fact is, it doesn't matter whether such a creature can even exist. We're talking here about mind deterrents—mental tricks that you can play on a prospective burglar. Appearances are the important thing, not reality, because appearances are what the burglar has to use to make his decision about whether it's safe to hit your house. The more you can do to make him think his life might be in danger if he even lingers around your place, the better the job you've done in protecting your home. Mental deterrents not only play havoc with the burglar's mind; they also tend to stop the burglar before he becomes an *intruder*—which means he won't even destroy a door or window. If you were a burglar and walked up to a door and saw a sign reading:

BURGLARS,

these aren't the best locks in the world,
and if you spend a little time at it,
you might even get in.
But I wanna tell you one thing.
You'd better take your last look at life,
because whether I'm home or not,
I've got something in here that
guarantees you won't
be coming out...*alive*.

I don't care how drunk or brave you are. When you're standing outside of somebody's home and read a sign like that, you don't need an I.Q. of 167 to realize it's best that you leave.

If you were to have two small signs made stating something like that, and put them on each door of your home, I'll bet you, you'd never have any trouble from burglars. The point is...MIND GAMES are ten times stronger than locks will ever be. Ask yourself this question: When you're driving along in your car and see a sign that says, "Intersection," what goes through your mind instantly? An intersection means a point where two or more roads meet and, if you don't pay close attention to what you're doing, you could be killed. Now that's something right there that most people are afraid of...being killed. So you've got to display some mental deterrents around your home that could make a burglar fear for his life.

The basic way to think about these mind games is to conceive of them as a method of talking to a burglar when you're not home. The dog dish—or just a few huge bones left lying by a door—tell him that there's some potential danger inside in a very specific way. The sign I mentioned does the same thing in a more ambiguous way.

Imagine a sign that said:

ATTACK DOGS
trained and sold here.

In the survey, 95 percent of the inmates said they'd be gone like a shot if they ran into this sign. The other 5 percent said they'd check it out further. Remember, "BURGLARY IS A MIND GAME." Only 65 percent said that dogs scared them away. I think it means something when a plastic sign scares away 95 percent and the dogs themselves only scare away 65 percent.

However, there's a right way and a wrong way to display these kinds of signs. The wrong way is to post them in your front yard in plain sight or nailed to the front of your house. That's advertising, and you're not doing that with these signs. At least that's not the intention. The right way is to put one on the outer gate of the fence going into the rear yard, and one on the other side. Post one on your back door and maybe on the front of your garage if it's to the rear of your house. Some people put the sign where passersby can see it. You'd think that's what you'd want, but it isn't. If it's out there in plain sight, it will give a burglar who cases the place time to watch and see if he ever sees any evidence of dogs. Whereas if he stumbles onto one of the signs in the dark of night, he's not doing to think of anything but how fast he can run. Household dogs are one thing, but "ATTACK DOGS" are something else. It wouldn't hurt to take a label marker and print up that sign and stick it on your outside front door, so daytime burglars can get a good look at it. Or go to a place that engraves signs and have a small one made up for your front door. Something that can't be read from the street.

Here's another one for those who don't believe until they see:

DANGER:

Extremely vicious
Barkless German Dobermans.

Believe me, in the frame of mind a burglar is in, while walking in people's yards, he is not going to pause to think for a second, "I wonder if there is such a thing." He's going to be gone. "Maybe there is...and maybe there isn't. But do I want to risk a piece of my hide to find out?" Every word in that sign means some form of danger to a person who is in your backyard (or wherever) when he has no-good in mind. These are only two of the many possible combinations of words that can be put together.

Consider a sign reading:

KNOCK ALL YOU WANT...

WE DON'T ANSWER THE DOOR.

Ninety-five percent of the inmates said they wouldn't mess with that house, typically commenting, "There are always other houses," or "I'd go next door." Five percent said they would stick around for a few minutes and either knock or throw small rocks at the windows. (I was amazed when I heard this about the rocks, because I had done this in my earlier burglary years.)

This is one of the most important mind games in the book, because it definitely works. The survey proves it, and plain common sense will tell you it can't help but work. It's a multifaceted mind game that will put the burglar's mind in a confused state, and 95 percent of burglars knock on doors or ring bells for the sole purpose of determining whether anybody is home. What could be easier for a burglar? Just walk up to any door...knock and, if nobody answers, hit the place.

Now if I were the kind of burglar who relied on door-knocking results and was staring at one of those signs, I'd probably still knock, but when no one answered, I wouldn't pronounce the house safe enough to hit. It doesn't take a very bright person to read this sign and realize that ringing the bell or knocking on the door is a total waste of time.

You ask, what about friends, relatives, and other people you're expecting? What happens when they knock? My answer: No problem! I didn't tell you not to answer the door. Answer the door all you want. But when you do, look out through a peephole with at least a 180° view of your doorway. And then if you positively know the person, answer the door. As soon as you see it's somebody you expect or want to see, let them in. Along with messing up a burglar's mind, the deterrent signs will also get rid of solicitors. When these signs are in place, they will only have cost pennies and will confuse burglars and give you more protection than any lock you can buy. Another great thing: even if a burglar knows the theory behind it, it doesn't help him a

damn bit. He still won't know if you're home playing games, or really out. If you're afraid that the
sign will achieve just the opposite... meaning if
you're afraid that, when you are actually home and
don't answer your door to someone you don't know,
they'll think you're out and still try the house, putting you into a possible face-to-face contact with
a burglar, then always answer your door. The sign
will still do its job when you're not home. That's
what its main purpose is in the first place... to
make someone think you could possibly be home
(when you're really not). It gives you protection
when you're home or when you're not home.

As I mentioned earlier, some aspects of burglar
alarm systems are in themselves mental deterrents: little signs that warn a burglar of potential
trouble. The most effective part of an alarm system
is the little decal that announces its presence. Another good mind deterrent is alarm foil stripped
along your windows. Both of these items tell a burglar that an alarm system is working here—even
if you don't have an alarm system! And again I'd
have a sign right where the phone line entered my
house. It would announce that if the line is cut,
the police will be summoned automatically. The
point here is not the truth or reality of the state-
ments; the point is that all these things instill fear
in a burglar.

As you'll see in the survey questions at the end
of this chapter, dogs are an excellent deterrent.
Although they rarely kept me away, there is something about a living, growling dog that sends a
burglar running. Fences can also be good deterrents, especially now that they can be equipped
with adjustable mercury vibration switches that
will trip your alarm system if someone tries to hop

over them. Alarm system decals and window foil can be very effectively used in cities on windows next to fire escapes. And a ten-cent alarm system decal on an apartment door is one of the best ways to make sure that a burglar will hit the unit next door, rather than yours. You might even want to install a dummy key pad on the wall next to your door.

You might be wondering here: What would have stopped me? Mind deterrents. If it was 89 degrees outside and everybody had their windows open, I stayed away. I hated fine gravel in driveways or rock gardens because there's no way to walk over it without making a racket.

Trip wires scattered around a yard posed a serious risk. At the same time, if I saw a Rolls or Mercedes parked outside a house, I couldn't pass it up. Don't fall for the old line that a parked car is going to keep burglars away because they'll think someone is home. They'll check anyway, especially if it's an expensive car. So stick it in a garage, out of sight.

And keep the garage locked. Once a burglar has gained entry to your garage, he is now well concealed and can stay as long as he wants, and do as much damage as he wants to break in. If that's not bad enough, more than likely the home owner's tools are right there on a workbench, ready for the burglar's use. Which simply means that with all this cover from sight and sound, and all the tools he needs, there is no lock around that will offer the resistance needed to keep him out.

There's only one thing you can do that will more than likely work. I'm talking about playing with the burglar's mind again. Somehow something must be done to make him think his life will be in danger should he open that door and enter. Now how can we do this? The only way is to tell him. And since you won't be there, you'll have to resort to the old sign method. There are a million things that could be written on a sign to do this. Here's the first one that came to my mind. It would have sent me off elsewhere if I had run into one during my burglary days.

Imagine: the burglar has gotten into your garage and has approached the door leading into your house. There, thumbtacked to the door is a piece of paper, *handwritten* with the following words:

CARPENTER

Please do not enter through this door

because my son's

3 rattlesnakes

have gotten out of the cage again

and we've closed them off in this room

we think, until he returns,

hopefully in a few days.

We're sorry for this inconvenience

but we don't want another person bitten

by them, as the first is still in the

hospital in intensive care.

Thank you.

Now you might think that there's no way this note is going to scare a burglar away. If you are one of those people who feel this way, then try just for a minute to put yourself in the position of a burglar walking up to a home and seeing that sign. Would you yourself want to take the chance of entering that door? As brave as I was, there's no way in hell I'd ever take the chance.

Tips on the note. It should *not* be typed, but rather printed very legibly so that your burglar can read it. Also it should be printed on one of those small white cards about six by eight inches and then tacked above and as close to the doorknob as possible. This way they can't help but see it.

One thing is for sure. If you don't use these notes, they definitely won't work. Like the time I had the flu in prison. I was really sick. I knew that bed rest was just what I needed, so I fought my way through red tape to be able to stay in my bed in the dorm, without being bothered by the personnel. I'd lie there with my eyes closed anyway and at least doze off. But not for long. Every other five minutes some—shall we say unkind inmate (to put it nicely)—would come up to me, tap the bunk and wake me up, asking for a match or to borrow the chair or whatever. So to cure the problem I tried my *mind games*, with a sign hanging at the end of my bed stating, "OUT OF ORDER, Please do not disturb." But it didn't work. There are always those of us who feel we're exempt from certain things (until we get caught). And besides, the sign offered no danger to them for messing with me.

So without advertising that all of my fingers had been sent out to foreign countries and individually trained in karate, I came up with another sign. It read, "CAUTION! At sick call, the doctor advised me that not only did I have the flu, but a mild case of the CRABS also. But don't worry. He said they were small and their leaping ability shouldn't be more than four feet." Well, I want to tell you, nobody bothered me for the remaining three days I was sick.

Now some of you might think: Oh come on, you want us to believe that the other inmates who read that sign believed it? I imagine there were some who knew the doctor wouldn't let me back in the dorm with crabs. But the thing is...WHY TAKE THE CHANCE?

Same with your house. It is so simple for anybody with three-fifths of a brain to sit down at home and make up a few clever word combinations, to scare the hell out of anybody wanting to mess with your residence. Then when you've got them on paper, either type them up or go someplace and have a couple of small signs printed and post them at both doors and a couple of windows. Here's another one I've made up without thinking to any great degree:

PLEASE STOP!

We've already been forced to kill one burglar

trying to get in while we weren't home,

so please don't become our second.

First of all, how did the people kill the burglar when they weren't home? No idea, right? Neither do I! But if I were outside of that house, I wouldn't want to stay around and find out. That one protects your home when you're out as well as in. Naturally if you have ways of killing him when you're out, you're very capable while at home, too.

Window Bars

I'll never forget the night I was walking around through yards searching for my next big score when I spied a house with bars on every window— the only house in the neighborhood with bars on the windows. Why? The house wasn't anything special. But they did have an alarm. And with the combination of the bars on the windows and an alarm...that did it. There must be something inside that house worth protecting! As I approached I checked the home's perimeter for anything suspicious. Everything looked all right, so I proceeded with my nine-point checklist (see pp. 118–119 for my checklist), making sure there was nobody home. Minutes later I had the alarm shut off and was still standing at the front door, where the outside on/off alarm plate was, when the owners pulled into the driveway. They didn't see me. At least I don't think they did. They weren't very sociable if they did.

I had to walk down the street still wondering what that residence had inside it to warrant bars on all its windows. I never did get to find out! The point of this story is that bars on windows *positively attract* burglars. It's a large neon sign saying, "We have something you want inside." I would never have given that house a second look if it hadn't been for those bars, for the house was well below the caliber of other homes I had been visiting.

Now I'm talking here about average suburban residential areas. There are obviously places in major cities where it would be crazy *not* to have bars. Of course, in these situations the bars are primarily there to keep potential assailants out when somebody is home inside. The bars are there to protect life, not property. And it's important to remember that this kind of defense is only as strong as its weakest link. You'll want a very secure door, certainly one with a chain. If you live in an apartment building, the main entrance should have two sets of doors, with an intercom just beyond the first set. An intercom is much more important than a doorman, who for the most part is undertrained, poorly paid and too easily distracted to do much good. It's the intercom that will help you be positive of the identity of anyone who seeks entry. It's also important that the second set of doors be extremely secure, because once a person is past the first set, all visibility from the street is usually cut off. And he has less to fear, which goes exactly counter to the concept of mind deterrents.

If you ever want to instill inspiration in a person to "go for it," bars will do it. What I mean by that is, bars are not going to stop a burglar from getting in. If he wanted to, all he'd have to do is tie a rope to them, have a friend back a car in, tie the rope to the bumper and floor it. They'd come off in a second. But in most cases he wouldn't even have to go to these extremes. Most houses that are barred have barless doors that still make easy pickin's. So not only are bars NEON SIGNS, but they are also not burglar stoppers. Worse than that, it makes a home a fire trap, should there ever be a blaze. I read recently in a Miami newspaper that someone burned to death in their own home when the bars on their windows prevented them from getting out.

Bars on windows always make burglars think that people have their life savings inside. And the bars only make the burglar more determined to get in. They're also characteristic of homes belonging to coin dealers and stamp dealers. Shutters will serve the same purpose, and somehow don't set off a burglar's mind. So if you're not going to feel safe until you've got something on your windows...make it shutters. Shutters are burglar-resistant, and can be opened from the inside in case of fire, and also provide added storm protection.

Security Patrols

I'm sorry to have to say here that security guards, neighborhood crime patrols and the like rarely offer much protection against good professional burglars. To a large extent, burglary is a battle of wits, and generally the people who patrol areas don't know what they're up against. Oh, they may be able to keep neighborhood kids from breaking into a house, but that's generally it. There is one notable exception: golf carts.

Golf Carts

Golf carts are very good for patrolling smaller areas. Condominiums, townhouses, and small residential communities sometimes utilize them for inexpensive, quiet operation. From a burglar's point of view they're thought of as "dangerous." In the past, I eluded many police cars and circling planes because of their operational noise. On the other hand, I was nearly caught several times by either police or security guards in golf carts. They are designed to be quiet, and they are. Once a burglar knows that certain areas are patrolled by golf carts, there's a good chance he will not work that area any longer.

Let's go to the survey now. There are a lot of good mental deterrents revealed in this set of questions:

Would dogs scare you away?

A. Sixty-five percent said that dogs of good size and unfriendly persuasion would scare them away. Thirty-five percent said they wouldn't, coming up with tales of the "poison steak," which I felt was just talk. Some said that, when they worked with friends, they'd have one guy keep the dog's attention, while the other guy broke into the home in another location, out of the dog's sight. My overall conclusion was that 90 percent of those who said dogs didn't scare them would actually have been shaking in their boots if the dogs came within twenty yards of them. As for myself—short and sweet—they didn't bother me 99 percent of the time.

Would "Beware of Bad Dog" signs scare you off?

A. Now we're back to the inexpensive mind games. The only problem is that this particular mind game is old hat. Every other house has a "Beware of Bad Dog" sign hanging somewhere and three-quarters of them are only used to scare off intruders. Hey... it's a great idea or should I say, it *was* a great idea, but maybe ten years ago. The survey says that only 25 percent was scared off by this sign, while 70 percent said it didn't faze them a bit. You need a more up-to-date sign now, like the "barkless Dobermans" mentioned earlier.

What kind of dogs scare you away the most?

A. This is a question a lot of you dog owners have wondered about. Shepherd owners are sure it's shepherds, while the Doberman owners know theirs are the most powerful mental deterrents around. And guess what? Doberman owners win. But only by 5 percent, with a total of 35 percent picking Dobermans as the dogs they'd least like to encounter. And I'm sorry, shepherd owners, it's not bad enough that you didn't take first place, but it's not even second or third. Second place are the owners of the "pit bulldog," with 30 percent saying that if they knew there was one of them around, they'd be gone. "All dogs" came in third, with 25 percent, and last was the "German shepherd" with 10 percent, saying the old police K-9 members still offer an unfriendly smile and a large bite.

Any way you look at it, dogs are a deterrent. Thirty-five percent of the inmates stated that dogs didn't bother them, but they bothered them enough so that the "poisoned steak" was mentioned by many. Something sure must be bothering them to have to take measures like that, wouldn't you say?

Even if you have only a tiny dog of some kind, they are still deterrents because of their bark. Burglars are afraid that the dog may arouse more than their bite. It is my opinion that small dogs (remember this is from first-hand experience) are the best watchdogs because their hearing seems to be better. I'll always remember the many times I would be walking through backyards and never be heard by large dogs, while it seemed the smaller ones could hear through walls. I owned toy poodles, but this has nothing to do with my opinion. Cats are even better than small dogs. They're incredible! Many times I'd walk past windows where home owners were sitting in a chair with their cats beside them. And the cats would either hear me or sense me. Boy, I sure was glad they couldn't talk.

If you can't have dogs for some reason or another, remember the dog signs. They're cheap and don't eat any more than a couple of thumbtacks. And, when you're at home sometime and your dog is barking and going crazy: he's trying to tell you something is wrong! I'm telling you . . . if I had a hundred dollars for every time I heard a dog owner tell their dog to "shut up . . . go lie down," while I was right outside their window, I'd be a millionaire. The dog is trying to tell you that somebody is outside, but you pay no attention. Yet when you think something is wrong you go running for your dog to check things out for you. Sure, there are false alarms. Sure, dogs bark at cats going by. But wouldn't you rather check his request out and be sure, than tell him to shut up and minutes later get robbed?

If you heard a TV or stereo on in a home as you were walking around it, but could not see in because of closed curtains, would you still hit the dwelling?

A. The purpose of this question is to find out if the longtime myth of leaving something going inside to make noise would actually scare the burglar away. I had 15 percent say that they would still hit the place after first knocking on the front door to see if anybody was home. The other 85 percent said they would leave. The key to the plan of noise in an unoccupied home is to make sure that no one can see inside even a tiny bit. The noise is only half the game; the complete curtain coverage is the other half. Your whole family should make a game of it and shut all the curtains in the entire house and then go outside and try to find the slightest space where anyone can see in. If there is one, your closed curtains have no effect at all.

Would you peek in garage windows to see if there were any cars present while checking out the home for the purpose of burglary?

A. I have done this many, many times and, you know, I really can't tell you why. You'd normally think it was to find out if there was anybody home. But whether there is one car there or three, it didn't really make any difference to me because I hit a house one time with eleven cars in the driveway, all obviously guests, but nobody at all was in the house. Where were they? You've got me. I was almost ready to quit for the night and go looking for them, but I didn't know how I would explain the police radios hanging from my belt—not to mention the gold and diamonds that were weighing me down, from that house and the one next door. However, I did look in the garage windows, as did 80 percent of the other inmates who took the survey. Twenty percent paid no attention. I would advise that you put roll-up shades on side garage windows and spray paint the insides of the door windows. Garage door windows serve no really important purpose but to aid a burglar planning to hit your home. They also enable him to get a good look at the door going from the garage into the house, which is a very weak point in a home's defense perimeter. Once they have broken into the garage, they can make all the noise they want and they can take whatever time they need to pick the lock on the house door, while remaining sheltered by your garage.

Did you knock on doors or ring doorbells to determine if people were home?

A. I would guess that burglars all over the world either knock on doors, or ring bells or something to that effect to determine if people are home. The survey shows that 95 percent said that they did use these methods of determining whether the residence was occupied. It is an absolute must for daytime burglary. Nighttime offers the concealment of darkness to venture between houses, to look in windows to see if anybody is home, but a final door check is still part of the whole business. Door knocking or bell ringing is a major tool for burglars to determine if a house is occupied.

Remember to post the sign discussed earlier: KNOCK ALL YOU WANT. WE DON'T ANSWER THE DOOR.

If the house you wanted to burglarize at night had spotlights lighting up the entire yard, would you still hit it?

A. Lights are a good deterrent, with only 30 percent answering yes. Seventy percent said they would not touch the place. Lights were only something that gave my gloves momentary warmth as I unscrewed them. They did not affect my operation. However, if you can afford the electric bill, leave them on. The survey shows they do help considerably.

Would you ever burglarize a home if there were no lights on inside or out?

A. Eighty-five percent said they would

and have hit houses while they were in total darkness. The other 15 percent joined me and said they wouldn't. I always figured if the people were so conservative that they couldn't keep a few lights on even during the daytime, then they were too conservative to have any jewelry or cash lying around. Besides, you can't break into a dark house and walk around without a flashlight, and that attracts too much attention.

I'll never forget the one time I tried it early on in my career. While covering the flashlight with my other hand, I walked slowly across the room sticking my foot into a bear's mouth. Well, how did I know the place was going to have a bearskin rug on its living room floor? Boy, I'm telling you, when I shone my light down on his head, noticing my foot was about gone, I turned and almost flew out of that house—knocking down everything in my way. The worst of it is the fangs got caught in my laces and I was pulling the bear with me, but I didn't realize that, until I just about clubbed it to death with my flashlight. That was my second night doing burglaries. Needless to say that was the last house I hit that night, and the last dark house I ever hit.

Would security guards (not police) deter you?

A. A lot of wealthy places today have their own little police forces called "security guards." Sometimes they are carrying guns, and sometimes they aren't, but they almost always ride around in police look-alike cars without the official blue or red lights. Do they scare off burglars? Well, it's hard to say. The results were fifty/fifty for this question. I have worked many areas while security guards roamed around in cars and on foot. What is most dangerous for the burglar is, as I've said, the use of golf carts.

Do yards that are fenced deter you?

A. Fences are one of the best things in the world . . . for keeping kids and dogs either in or out of your yard, dividing property and things of that nature. But they aren't worth a damn when it comes to burglars, trespassers or anybody else who wants to get into your yard. Ninety-five percent stated that they don't hesitate to climb over fences, while only 5 percent said they wouldn't bother. If you feel secure behind that fence, you're only tricking yourself.

What would scare you away from a residence more than anything?

A. Fifty-nine percent said that people in the house would scare them away from a home more than anything. Second choice was man's best friend...a dog, with 32 percent of the inmates saying that almost all dogs scared them away. The other 9 percent pertains to nighttime burglaries only: spot- or floodlights lighting up the yard. So your best deterrent is being at home, and since you can't stay at home all your life, try posting a few dog signs.

Would you enter a home from the front, back or sides?

A. A whopping 72 percent picked the back of any place to make their entrance. It offers the most protection for the burglar, away from the street and other houses. Twenty-six percent would rather break in through the sides of your home while only 2 percent picked the front.

This question might not show you anything you already didn't know but it confirms it if nothing else. Light up the rear of your yard, and use *mind deterrents*.

If you were to see signs of life in homes on either side of the house you're hitting, what would you do?

A. Only 44 percent of the inmates said

this would be enough of a deterrent for them to leave, while the other 56 percent said they would stay and continue to burglarize the place. Unfortunately, it usually takes something like this to get the other families (that were home) to realize that it could have happened to them. Having been spared, they will build up their home protection plan by replacing burned out spotlights, putting up newer ones, etc. As I think I stated before, we all have that tendency to wait until it happens to us, whatever it may be, before we take action. We all learn the hard way.

As you're walking into a yard of a house you intend to burglarize and approach a fence gate that is closed, would you open it and go in or pass and leave if that was the only way in?

A. Seventy-nine percent stated that they wouldn't think twice about going in after opening the fence gate. I would have loved to have seen what they would have done while standing outside of my seven-foot non-see-through fence where, on the only gate, I had a sign reading, "BEWARE RABID DOGS INSIDE." I'm telling you, my home was the only one where meter readers would always knock on the front door first, so I could bring the diseased animals inside the house.

The other percentages were divided up with 7 percent saying that they wouldn't go in, while 14 percent said they might go in. This is a good example of where other *mind deterrents* would make the difference.

In the same situation as in the last question, if the gate is now locked, would you hop over it or say the heck with it and leave?

A. Now, with it locked, only 55 percent would hop over, while there were 79 percent who would have just walked in if it was unlocked. Twenty percent stated that they would not mess with it at all and leave, and 25 percent said that they might hop over it. The reason is that they'd be afraid someone might see them hopping over a gate, which is a good indication that something suspicious is going on. As you can see, although it's troublesome, it helps if you lock your gate. It's up to you. Do you want to keep your grandmother's heirloom pendant or let some burglar take it, crush it into pieces and sell it for scrap gold?

If you were burglarizing an area and came upon a residence with storm shutters on all of the windows, would you attempt to burglarize that house? In

other words, would you attempt removing the shutters to gain entry?

A. Shutters offer a tremendous amount
of protection to people who have them on
their homes. One hundred percent of the
inmates stated that they wouldn't spend
the time trying to break into a residence
that had them. They're either too noisy or
too time-consuming.

I was only doing burglaries a short time
when I decided that I needed the protection on my home that the shutters offered.
When I went out at night doing burglaries,
I did my window shopping at residences
with their goods already displayed and in
use. You'd be surprised at the number of
items I bought after testing them out in
homes. Color TVs, stereos, furniture, fences
for my yard and even shutters had many
trial runs before I purchased them for my
own home. That's how I happened to pick
Rolladen shutters. I'd seen them on more
houses than others, so I walked up and
examined them one night, crowbar at
hand. I wasn't there for any more than a
few seconds when I knew it would be a
waste of time trying to bypass them. A day
later I called the Rolladen dealer in Ft. Lauderdale, who came to my house, and
within five weeks my home was clad in
these unbeatable shutters. I had three of
the window shutters motorized, so with
a flip of a switch they went up and down,

while others were hand-operated and worked very easily. Along with feeling more secure from burglary, I felt 200 percent better whenever there was a storm in the area. Anybody who can afford shutters should have them installed. It's an instant mind deterrent, even from a distance. I only picked Rolladen because they are the best, but there are others around.

Superthief M.O. Checklist

Here is the checklist that I used before entering any home. On the left side of the page is the Superthief checklist. On the right is a summary of what can be done, when possible, to foil any burglar trying to repeat these actions.

1. Does place look worth hitting? Value of any cars present, etc.

If you're reading this book, your home is worth hitting.

2. Visual check of the windows. Look inside to see if anyone is home, and at the same time look for any indications of an alarm. If no one is seen, pro-

Make sure it is impossible for any potential burglar to see into any part of your home. Make sure there are plenty of indicators— decals, window sen-

ceed. If an alarm is indicated then go to step three.

sors, etc.—that there is an alarm system, whether or not you actually have one.

3. Alarm switch: Locate the alarm system's turn-off switch and find out whether or not the system can be turned off. If it can't be—because it's a digital pushbutton type, or because it's inside the home—then go on to the next house. If the alarm can be turned off, then go to step four.

Make sure any alarm system is internally controlled, i.e., the on/off switch is NOT mounted outside a door or in a driveway.

4. Turn off alarm. If it was done before verifying no one was home, someone could have been inside and caught you messing with their alarm. When alarm is off, go on to step five.

Same as in step three.

5. Choose the easiest way in. It could be a door or a window but, whichever it is, make sure it's not so close to a neighbor's house that, if a noise is made, it will be heard.

Nothing can be done to prevent this. No matter how well you've attempted to protect all possible entrances, if a burglar is determined to get in, he will choose what appears to him to be the *least* troublesome way into your particular house.

6. Before going further, knock on the door or tap on the window. This will not only bring someone to life if they are at home, but it will also bring to life the family dog, if there is one. Peek in to see what kind of dog you are up against.

Make sure your door has one of the signs, discussed earlier in this chapter, that will scare away 99 percent of the burglars working.

7. Before opening the door or window, pick the escape route that you will be able to sprint with the least amount of obstacles. Have all your tools and whatever else you've got with you together, so if for any reason something happens, you won't leave anything behind.

Little can be done here, other than turning your front and back yards into obstacle courses.

8. Go ahead and do what has to be done to get in, making as little noise, and as little mess, as possible. Once inside, pick up the phone and listen for an

Make sure the house has heavy-duty locks, doors and window shutters that will create a lot of noise if tampered with. A leased telephone line will also

alarm tape going out. If it is, take action by hanging up and leaving phone off hook. Then go and learn all the ways out, making sure the doors can be opened and that you are not trapped in there if someone comes home.

thwart any interference with the phone or the phone lines. The telephone line sign discussed earlier in this chapter is also effective against burglars.

9. Before going to work, do a radio check making sure you can reach your driver, and vice versa, and that everything's all right. Then check your police radio, making sure you are on the right channel and they are coming in clear. Pay attention for any dispatches to your location, which would indicate that a silent or secondary alarm has been triggered.

Nothing can be done to prevent this.

CHAPTER 5

WHERE TO HIDE WHAT YOU VALUE

Most burglars, once they have broken into a home, head right for the master bedroom. I certainly did, and 95 percent of the inmates surveyed said the same thing. So it's obvious that you don't want to keep valuable things in the bedroom, with a few possible exceptions. It's reasonably safe to tuck things into handbags, if there are 20 bags sitting in a closet. The same is true of shoe boxes, if there are thirty or forty of them stacked up. I never liked to go into a house and dump everything out, so these are good places to conceal things. On the other hand, if you're hit by a dumper, you've got a problem.

There aren't that many totally safe places to hide things, aside from locking them up in a floor safe. There are places you definitely *shouldn't* use to hide your valuables. Any drawer that slides out is a bad place, as is any cabinet that has a hinged door. Burglars will always check them. We saw earlier in the survey that medicine chests are bad places. Another bad place is in those phony electrical outlets that are being sold through magazines and catalogues. Every burglar knows about them now.

It's not a bad idea to bury valuable things in your back yard. And it's also not too risky to hide things in a dropped ceiling—the kind that's hung from joists, with the removable pieces lying on metal strips. The police missed over $30,000 I had in my ceiling. Cutting out the inside of a book is fairly sensible, although some guys will pull every book from a shelf just to see if anything falls out. It depends partly on how many books you have. I can also tell you that not many burglars will look behind or underneath upholstered chairs and couches, when the fabric extends to the floor.

Again here, remember mind games. Give a burglar something to take. I used to keep a few hundred dollars worth of junk jewelry on top of my dresser. A lazy burglar will grab that and think he's got it all.

Small bags of jewelry can be stuck in the pockets of clothes hanging in closets. Living room or dining room closets are best. Kitchen cabinets and other places in the kitchen are bad. But clothes dryers or washing machines or laundry hampers are fairly safe places to stow away what you don't want a burglar to take.

I think it's worthwhile to engrave things—

Floor Safe.

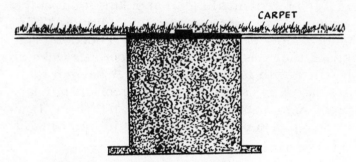

Floor Safe Installed in Cement Below Floor Level.

deeply—with your social security number. It'll give some guys second thoughts about taking your stuff. Fences don't like it, and at least it does help in retrieving the stolen goods. And you might try marking things with invisible ink that shows up only under a black light. In this case the mind deterrent is important. You might have signs on the doors notifying potential burglars: "All valuables in this house are encoded with invisible identification marks."

But from all my experience and from watching the police tear my own house apart, I'd have to say the best place to hide things is in a floor safe. (That is, a safe that's sunken into the floor with a carpet over it.) And the best room in the house to put the safe would be in the living or dining room in the corner under the carpet. Those two rooms are rarely given much attention by a burglar other than to grab the silverware.

The method for installing a floor safe is to have a safe company come to your house with an *air* chisel. They dig a hole about two feet deep in the cement and bury the safe with new cement around it. There's a square plate welded onto the bottom of it to prevent anything from pulling it out of the cement. The house can entertain a hundred burglars, a fire can level the place, or a bulldozer can knock the walls down, and the floor safe will still be there with its contents intact. What you want are class E or F safes: they're fireproof and burglarproof. Forget about wall safes. I can't tell you how many I pulled out and lugged off to the trunk of my car.

And now, to the inmates...

What would you say are the best places for hiding valuables? Where were the places that you wouldn't spend time searching?

A. Eighty-one percent stated that safes of good quality were hiding places that they didn't bother messing with. They're speaking about safes of good quality. That means if one burglar can pick it up and lug it out of your residence while smoking a cigarette, it's not good quality. That would be called a burglar's delight. Why? Because they know you had enough faith in it to purchase it in the first place, so you must have had enough faith in it to use it to store your valuables. Easy pickin's! *Safes are only as safe as their installations.* Second choice was hiding things, in this case money, in a book and putting the book on a shelf with many other books. It's too time consuming to bother with.

Where would you look first for the goods in a residence?

A. This was almost another landslide victory, with 95 percent stating that as soon as they would enter a home, or apartment, or condominium or whatever kind of residence they were burglarizing, the master bedroom would be the first place to look for the goods. I fell into that category, too, stepping into a home and walking right past any and everything to get to the master bedroom. It's the worst place in the world to hide anything of great value.

Second choice was the living room/dining room with 4 percent. Here a burglar would run into a color TV, stereo equipment, small electronic gadgets, and of course the silverware. Not only is silverware a problem because of its monetary value, but it's also hard to conceal. What can you do about it? The only two things I can recommend are to either install an alarm system in your home, or buy a nice big safe and store the silverware there. Both are expensive, but so is the value of your silver.

While in a closet, usually in a master bedroom, if a woman had several dozen shoe boxes on shelves and the same number of out-of-date handbags hanging somewhere in the closet, would you take the time to go through every one of them?

A. Only 20 percent said they would, while 80 percent said they wouldn't take the time to go through them. Whatever it is you're hiding, it has a pretty good chance of surviving a burglary in one of these two places. I myself would spend as long as I wanted in a home looking, but never spent the time even at one house to go through all of those bags with all of their compartments. Almost every house I visited had a minimum of ten bags and fifteen shoe boxes piled somewhere. Fair hiding place.

Have you ever looked under the mattress or under beds for anything?

A. This is one of the worst places that a person can hide something. Ninety percent stated that they looked under beds and in between mattresses. I have found many ladies' handbags with cash inside them slipped under beds, along with guns, clubs, vibrators, and dirty magazines. I never did a job during which I wouldn't check under the beds. It's a bad place to put anything but dust and slippers.

Would you check refrigerators or freezers for anything of value?

A. Since so many burglars are into drugs, this is a very popular place to look, because some drugs are kept in the freezer. Ninety percent said they look in both of these places. I never checked—although when I was thirsty, I might go for an ice-cold ginger ale or Pepsi, and a dish of ice cream was always good in the midst of things.

While in a home, in a closet, would you take time to go through every single pocket of the clothes hanging up?

A. Thirty-five percent said yes, which is hard to believe. If they even saw some of the walk-in closets I've seen—that looked like clothing stores—they would have needed sleeping bags. The other 65 percent said they wouldn't go through them all. I would hide anything in a pocket of a rack full of clothes, provided there were at least thirty garments hanging in that closet, which is well under what the average person has. I feel it's a safe place. Clothing hanging over a chair or draped across something is just the opposite. Never leave anything of value in those pockets.

Would you take the time to go through every shoe that is found in the average closet?

A. For some reason there was a 5 percent increase over those who said they would spend the time to check out the clothes pockets. Forty percent said they would sit there on the floor in your closet and check through every single shoe for valuables. Having seen Thom McCann's warehouse in many home closets, I wouldn't waste the time. However, I don't feel as safe about this one, as with the pockets. I wouldn't hide anything in shoes anywhere.

Did you ever pull books off a shelf, looking for valuables inside?

A. Only 25 percent stated that they have pulled a few books off shelves at times and gone through them. Seventy-five percent said that it takes too much time.

What would you steal first?

A. Seventy-eight percent picked the combination of jewelry and money. This was also the category that I would have been in. Anything else was a waste of time. Eleven percent chose electrical appliances, which means just about anything that plugs in: TVs, stereos, video equipment, clock radios, toaster ovens. Six percent concentrated on furniture, antiques, pictures and the larger items that require a truck of some kind. And last were the 5 percent who picked drugs.

Did you ever steal liquor from a home during a burglary?

A. Just about everybody's home has some alcohol in it, whether it's beer, wine or the hard stuff. The survey shows that 60 percent of the burglars will steal your liquor. The other 40 percent are going to leave it behind so you can get loaded and forget your losses.

Would you take TVs, radios, stereos, etc. if, as you were picking them up, you saw I.D. numbers engraved on them?

A. Seventy-five percent said they would take them anyway. Engraving I.D. numbers on property does not prevent your local burglar from taking it, but it does help in the recovery of your property. So it is a very good idea to engrave, or in some way mark your property, either with your social security number or your name and address. Equipment for doing this is at your police station and local crime-watch headquarters.

I did not take property other than jewelry or cash.

Would you steal guns from inside a home?

A. Another landslide. Ninety percent of the 300 inmates said yes, they would steal guns whenever they found them. Citizens all over the world buy guns for their protection at home and a good percentage of them are stolen from their own homes, and used for robberies, gang fights, murder and every other crime committed with guns. What good is a gun if it's not near your bed, right? But you saw earlier that hiding things under beds and in between mattresses is useless. That leaves end tables on each side of the bed. I always checked those places, frequently finding guns there. Where should you hide guns? Good question! I would say on the floor, behind a dresser or chair. I never looked there, and in my many discussions with burglars I have never heard of anybody else looking there. Put the weapon by your bed at night and hide it every morning. It wouldn't take any more time than slipping the old dentures back in.

What do you do with the stuff after you get it?

A. The first choice was the burglar's best friend...his fence, with 65 percent choosing that for an answer. Second place was a legal business doing illegal business...the pawn shop, with 22 percent of the vote. The rest—13 percent—sold the goods to friends or anybody they could.

If you were in a house and for some reason were pressured into getting out fast and only had time to take one piece of electronic equipment, what would you take?

A. Naturally a burglar is going to grab whatever is handy under these conditions, but this question was designed to show you what electronic items get taken most often. First choice, with 45 percent, is the household stereo. It's going! They're easy and fast sellers from what I'm told. Second on the list of most-wanted items is video equipment: recorders, cameras, and the like, with only a slight difference of 43 percent. Then to attach to their recently acquired video recorder comes the family's color TV. I mean how are they going to watch what the recorder has recorded? Mark your property well with engravers, or other methods suggested by local police.

Best and Worst Hiding Places

FAIR HIDING PLACES	POOR HIDING PLACES
Buried containers	Master bedrooms in general
Dropped ceilings	Any sliding drawer
Washing machines	Any cabinets with hinged doors
Clothes dryers	Phony electrical outlets
Garbage cans	Medicine chests
Hollowed-out books	Under mattresses
Behind and under unupholstered chairs	Refrigerators and freezers
In pockets of clothes hanging in a closet	In pockets of clothing draped across a chair
In handbags stored in closets	

CHAPTER 6

BEFORE YOU GO AWAY

Most burglars don't want a confrontation. They want it easy. They'd like to be able to spend as much time as they want in your house, turning the place upside down to find every last item of value.

Think about that for a minute. They don't just want to hit your place when you're out. They'd like to hit it when you're away—off on vacation, with no chance of walking in while the crime is in progress.

Unfortunately too many people give burglars an opportunity to know exactly when they're away.

135

There are obvious things like newspapers piling up. And there are more subtle giveaways. If your lights have been left on timers, and the power goes out, it becomes pretty clear that nobody's home. Lights on in the daytime are a neon sign. Once when I was going through my checklist, I called a telephone only to hear an answering machine announcing that the family was on vacation in the Caribbean for three weeks. I don't have to tell you that their house became an instant target. Not only did I know they wouldn't be home that night; I presumed that if they had enough money for the whole family to go away that long, they had enough things around the house that would be worth taking. I left them a thank-you note for telling me they had been away, and said I hoped they had had a nice time and hadn't gotten too sunburned.

All I'm suggesting here is that you not make it obvious that you're away. Some of the mental deterrents are useful here, such as the "Knock All You Want..." sign. Here's a checklist to run down before you go away for more than a day:

1. Have adult neighbor pick up your mail, newspapers, and advertising materials. *DO NOT* ADVISE POSTAL DEPARTMENT OR NEWSPAPER OFFICE OF YOUR VACATION.

2. The night before you leave, close all curtains, so that *not one* window in the residence leaves the *smallest peephole* to see in—then go outside *your own house* and try to see in. If you can, fix it so you can't. Then leave it secure until you get home.

3. Use lights set on alternating timers.

4. Leave at least one radio on fairly loud and near a back window; two radios if possible. They draw little current.

5. Don't advise lawn maintenance or any utility company that you will be gone.

6. Take very valuable jewelry and silver over to the house of a relative or good friend.

7. Have *outside lights* on a light-sensitive switch, *NOT* a timer. You know someone's away if their outside lights are on during the day. And don't use outside lights that can be unscrewed.

8. If possible have a neighbor empty a small trash can of junk into your empty trash canister so it will appear even to your sanitation department that you are home.

9. Take your phone off the hook. Anyone who calls will think someone's home. This also prevents the dead giveaway to a burglar that nobody's home: hearing the phone ring and no one answers it.

10. Lock all doors and windows.

11. Turn on alarm system.

Anytime you leave your home unoccupied for any length of time, before you leave:

1. Lock all doors and windows.

2. Take phone off hook.

3. Close curtains.

4. Leave radio on.

5. Leave lights on inside if there is any chance of being gone into the night.

6. Utilize all signs.

7. Leave no notes on door or in mailbox.

Here's what the inmates had to say about how they determined whether homeowners were absent.

Would you look for newspapers left on the lawn and mail building up in the mailbox as signs of no one being home?

A. These are things that are talked about at crime-watch programs all over the country, yet people still don't do anything about them. They come home from a trip and their mailbox is spilling over and the lawn looks like a new city dump ...and the house has been broken into. Guess whose fault that is? You're right ...it's yours. You're advertising again. Advertising usually gets results no matter what you're selling. My survey shows that 60 percent of the burglars did look for these two items as signs of no one being home. The other 40 percent said they never gave it much thought.

Did you look in the newspapers for fu-
neral or wedding announcements to see
when the people would be out, and then
hit those houses?

A. Eighty-five percent of the inmates
never did this while 15 percent said they
had. I never have, although they tried to
pin this on me when I was arrested. I don't
believe it's as common as it's thought to
be. However, as you can see, it is done.
The only thing you can do, along with
utilizing all of the other mind games
you've read about so far, is to have somebody who gets too upset at weddings and
funerals stay at your house during these
times. There are always a couple in every
family.

Would you ever get names off the front
of the home or a mailbox, look the people
up in the phone book and then call them
to see if they were at home?

A. This is something that I don't think
too many people are aware of—or in some
cases they are aware of it, but don't think
it applies to them. Or they just spent fifty
dollars to have a nice new sign made up
with their name and address on it along
with all of the kids' names and they're not
about to do away with it just because

somebody might look up the phone number and call to verify that they're not home. These signs must go.

The survey showed that 45 percent said they did do this, while 55 percent didn't.

Do you agree that the large garbage containers that the city picks up a few times a week, when left in the front of the house after they've been emptied, are signs that people are not at home?

A. How many of you thought of this one? See how a burglar's mind works. My containers at home were emptied at 7:30 A.M. If I had left before that, which often happened, and was gone for a good part of the day, I'd find that mine and maybe one or two others were the only ones left at the curb. A dead giveaway to daytime burglars. If you work, and can't be there to put the container back in your yard, have a neighbor do it for you. It would only take them a few minutes. Then make them a plate of brownies to show your appreciation. "What goes around—comes around." I know that well. Sixty-five percent said that they always looked for this along with other advertisements like the mail and newspapers. The other 35 percent of the inmates surveyed worked only at night, as I did, and this wouldn't play any part in night burglaries.

Do you think that advertising materials or samples hanging either on door knobs or in the door jamb are an indication of people being out?

A. Another high score with 90 percent saying these are good indications of nobody being home. Now I'm not talking about these items when they've just been dropped off. I'm talking about them building up over a period of time or a burglar watching them being delivered early in the morning and seeing them still lying there at 3:30 that afternoon. Another definite giveaway that nobody is at home: when U.P.S. and other delivery services have been there, found you weren't home, and then left their little note on your door saying, "Sorry we missed you," etc. They might as well plant a flag in your front yard saying THESE PEOPLE ARE NOT HOME. A mail slot in the door would solve this problem. One burglar told me that he used to follow about six houses behind the people passing out samples and pick them up as they were left. Then he would go to the places he wanted to hit, delivering the samples and knocking on doors at the same time to see who was home.

As signs of nobody being at home, did you ever look for a note taped to the door?

A. Speaking of advertising! This is about the worst thing you can do to inform a burglar that the place is vacant. I remember one night I found a note on a door saying something to the effect of "Hey, Joe . . . we're over at the Wilsons." At which time I ran down my nine-point checklist just to be sure there was no one home, turned the alarm off, went in, borrowed on a long-term basis about sixty thousand dollars in jewelry, left, turned the alarm back on again so no other burglars would go in and mess up the place, and on the same note hanging on the door, left a message saying, "Sorry I missed you, be back another time."

Don't advertise that no one is home. You're asking . . . almost begging for trouble by flying that piece of paper on your door. The survey shows that 72 percent of the inmates looked for notes of this type. Some people even have special little note pads right by their doors.

Would you ever get tips that people weren't home and, if yes, from whom?

A. Fifty-one percent said that they got their tips from their friends. Twenty-four percent stated that they got a lot of their tips from their "fence" about where the good houses were, etc. Eighteen percent picked up their best tips from the service-men that work in neighborhoods, like the lawn maintenance people, garbage men, meter readers, etc. Be careful whom you tell that you're not going to be home, and remember that these people might look trustworthy, but burglars come in all different styles and colors. Five percent said that they never got any tips at all, just got lucky while walking around. And the one I was most annoyed at for passing out information about absence was the mailman. Even though it's only 2 percent, I was surprised to hear that some mailmen would aid burglars by telling them who is home and who isn't. I wonder what else they would do? And who would know better than a mailman, being able to walk up to any door he wants without any suspicion at all. Here again, it shows the value of the mail slot in the door for the purpose of *not having* to advise the mailman when you're going to be away.

The fewer people you let know of your trips, the safer you'll be.

CHAPTER 7

PRIME TIME
FOR BURGLARS

Luckily for the sake of insurance companies and jewelry owners alike, New Year's Eve only comes around once a year. It is a known fact that this is the best night of the year for burglars. Why? Even the stay-at-homes splurge on this night and go out to dinner, go to a family get-together, or party to bring in the new year. Half the fun of the evening is staying out till the old year is gone and the new year arrives, which means midnight, or in other words a long working night for the burglar with not too much chance of anybody coming home. It also means in some cases that the people who keep the best of their jewelry at the bank have brought it home for the night. This gives the burglar his one chance in the year to acquire what didn't get picked out for the evening's flash. I know. I've found plenty of stuff lying around on New Year's Eves that wouldn't have been there on other nights.

So we have almost everybody going out and staying out until at least 12:30 A.M., and more than likely some good jewelry in the residence. That's a winning combination. On this night in particular you should take special care to bunk anything valuable in a place you feel confident will be overlooked, just in case three or four uninvited guests come wandering through your house to tear it apart. Whatever you do, don't leave anything in your bedroom closets on New Year's Eve, or your new year could start off on the wrong foot. Make sure that all of your curtains are completely closed and leave a stereo on fairly loud—maybe another one on upstairs, if you have an upstairs. Splurge on my ideas for this night, even if you don't use them the rest of the year. You've got a good chance of getting hit on New Year's—it's the one night of the year that 99 percent of the burglars are out there gathering up treasures. They know that there's always another night for a party.

There are actually a lot of periods that can be identified as prime time for burglars. Smart ones, for instance, will find out when the local police force changes shifts. When that happens, there tend to be fewer squad cars out on the street. So it won't hurt you to know the same information, and be more careful at those times. Burglars also love it when there's a huge fire or other disaster in the general vicinity. That way the cops are off paying attention to civil needs, thus giving the burglar a better chance of not getting caught.

The reality is, as the survey questions indicate, that pretty much any time is a good time for a burglary. But some times are more popular than others, and that's when you've got to make sure that most of the deterrents already discussed are properly deployed.

Here's what the inmates said:

Did you do burglaries in the day or at night?

A. Fifty-five percent of the inmates said that they preferred daytime burglaries over the 45 percent who chose the concealment of darkness. As for myself, there was no way I ever would have done a burglary in the daylight.

The figures are close enough, as far as I'm concerned, to say that you must be on guard twenty-four hours a day. Just because there are two types of burglars doesn't mean that they work in special areas. This means that a day or night burglar could enter your neighborhood any time he wants. Always be alert and on the defensive.

What would you consider the best time for doing burglaries?

A. As shown in the previous question, daylight burglaries were favored over nighttime burglaries by a 10 percent lead.

This question shows what time in the day you are most likely to be hit. Fifty-nine percent stated that for daytime burglaries they would work between 8 A.M. and 12 noon. With 26 percent of the vote, the second most popular time coincided with my time schedule: between 5 P.M. and 9:30 P.M. Third most popular was again at night, with 7 percent working between 9:30 P.M. and 12 midnight. Fourth choice with 4 percent was the midnight-on crew. In my estimation these are the most dangerous hours, both for you and the burglar. He knows you're home asleep and is relying solely on his CREEPING ability to carry him from rags to riches. But what happens if you wake up and hear him in your house? We've already discussed the O.K. Corral situations, and you know now that you don't want to precipitate that problem. I'd get out of bed and say in a loud voice, so the burglar could hear me in the next room or wherever, "Hey honey, you're positive this shotgun is loaded?" Or maybe "Yeah, but this machine gun is going to mess up our walls." Hey . . . let me tell you something. This guy, no matter how stoned he might be, is going to be tripping over himself trying to get out of that house. And I'll bet he's not particular about which window he jumps through.

Now let's look at what you've done. You've learned how to talk to yourself (if alone) but most important you've saved your life and your kids' lives. You haven't caught the intruder, but...Ah Hah!!! It sure would be a good time for a horn blast, wouldn't it, now that he's on the outside! Now you call the police... if you can.

I can't vouch for this first-hand. I'm only imagining myself as a former burglar in the position of hearing these lines, and telling you how it would affect me. I'd be gone faster than a speeding bullet. And I'm also giving you my idea of what I would do if I was awakened by this. One other choice, and it's very risky, is to pretend you're asleep and pray that they do not want to mess with you. I couldn't do that one myself.

The remaining 4 percent of the inmates did burglaries between 12 noon and 5 P.M.

Which nights of the week would you consider best for burglary?

A. I'm pretty sure the FBI statistics show that more burglaries occur on Saturday nights than any other night of the week. This was also the case with my survey. Saturday night took 52 percent of the votes, Friday night took 22 percent, and Sunday night 19 percent, with week nights capturing the remaining 7 percent.

Now let me talk a little about each. Saturday night is the best night for burglars because that's the night that all senior citizens go out and play cards. It's the night that many people go out to eat, and basically it's just known as the most fun night of the week for parties, movies, first dates and burglaries. It was my best night of the week. Friday was a very close second. It was second because—as the inmates all agreed—it was payday, the day everybody was out spending some of that hard-earned money. However, it was also a working day and people were always tired from the day's work, which called for an earlier curtailing of intrusions. But as I got more knowledgeable, my areas changed from the working, payday locations, to the retirement and millionaire neighborhoods.

Sunday night comes up third in popularity. This was a night that I never worked, meaning I never did a burglary. You're probably wondering why? Well, for some reason, I just couldn't bring myself to strap on the radios and work this day. I knew it was a good day for burglaries, with all the Sunday dinners and family get-togethers, but still I had an agreement with somebody, as strange as that sounds.

In general, weekends are the best times for being burglarized. This excludes the Thanksgiving and Christmas holidays. During the holiday season, you stand a good chance of getting hit any night of the week until after January 2, when things taper off just a bit.

Would you rather have rainy weather or nice weather for doing burglaries?

A. I preferred rainy, windy, lousy nights for doing burglaries. It covered up the noise if any was made, the footprints if any could be left, and made for poor aftermath investigation work, along with poor visibility from cars. Besides, what police officer really wants to get out of a warm dry car to get wet? There are a few, but for the most part they would rather stay dry. Fifty-five percent agreed with my way of thinking.

The other 45 percent were fair-weather burglars. So even though you can get hit any time, don't rule out rainy days or nights. Burglars don't have holidays or rain dates. They'll work any time.

How long would you spend in a home?

A. This was divided into four answers. Forty percent said that they would stay in a place they had just burglarized under thirty minutes, while a close second of 35 percent would only stay in your place for fifteen minutes. The third runner-up was 20 percent staying in the house as long as they felt like it. That's the category I would have fallen into. Sometimes, if I was hungry, I would even eat there, but I always cleaned up after myself, putting the dishes in the dishwasher, etc. The remaining 5 percent would only stay in the place for up to an hour, and then call it quits. What does this question tell you? That burglars today take their time. There's no rush. So you've got to hide that stuff well or it will be found.

How many houses would you hit in one night or day?

A. Ninety-two percent said that they hit between one and five residences per day or night. Only 8 percent said that they hit between six and ten places in that same time period. So if you just got home, and in some way could determine that your place had been hit just a short while ago, chances are that the burglar is still in your neighborhood. He might even still be inside. So leave until the police get there. Call the police from next door. Another important point is that if you have walked into your home and it has just been burglarized: *don't touch anything.* Even though most burglars wear gloves, there's still a chance that the police might pick up on prints or clues, if you don't mess things up. And there's always the slim chance that the burglar is coming back to pick up a few things he couldn't haul away on the first trip.

CHAPTER 8

WHAT OTHERS COULD DO

We've been concentrating here on what you can do to make your house safe. And obviously YOU can do more than anyone else in that regard. You know the strengths and weaknesses of your own home, and by now you hopefully realize that you can't really depend on anyone else to protect your house.

But there are a few things that other people— and I'm speaking of public institutions here— could do to make all our homes safer.

The phone company could help prevent burglaries. Earlier I mentioned leased lines, which send a signal when cut.

It seems to me that all lines could be leased lines, in effect. It's vitally important to know if your phone line has been cut. It's generally the one link we have to the outside world. One way would be to have a small red light on the phone itself (something like the message light they have in hotels and motels), telling the home owner that his phone line is inoperative. It could even have a little buzzer or beeper of some sort. It should also be possible to have a system where a cut line lights up a light, beeps a beeper and prints out the number of the line that has been cut right at the phone company itself. Sound difficult? Ma Bell already has digital screens in front of operators in large cities, where as soon as a phone line anywhere is connected with the operator, it displays the phone number on the screen. In other words if you live in a city of any size and you dial the operator, just as soon as she or he answers, your number is flashed on a screen in front of them.

What you can ask the phone company *to do now* is to raise the entrance point, at which the phone lines enter your home, out of anyone's reach. And if they're at heights already beneficial to them, then at least encase the wires in conduit—heavy tubing that holds wires. Both maneuvers would make it tougher for burglars to cut phone lines.

I've approached millionaires' homes where they had spent money to have the phone lines buried underground, where they entered the home through the basement wall. It would be nice if all phone lines were buried from the pole to the house. For if you will only stop and think of it, when you're in any kind of trouble at all, you run right to your phone, and it's nice to have it working.

These same ideas could be applied by power companies. If the power line is cut before it hits the cut-off box or meter, it would sound an alert back at the generator or switching station.

I've approached both phone and power companies about these ideas. Their main objection has been that if a car were to hit a utility pole, 500 alarms would be sounded by the severed circuits. That always seemed so simplistic to me. Obviously if the 500 alarms were all coming from the same area—and they'd know that—then the problem had to be with a utility pole or a downed line.

What do we call them? PUBLIC utilities?

The only other things that have always bothered me are mailboxes. I can understand that it sometimes would be tough for mailmen to approach every home from the street, rather than just lean out of the truck and stuff the box full of letters, bills, magazines and parcels.

Still, letter slots on doors would make it much tougher for would-be burglars to know that you happen to be away.

Police headquarters ought to utilize more marked cars in patrolling neighborhoods. As we've seen earlier, it doesn't do any good to conceal the fact that you have a burglar alarm. And from a deterrent standpoint, it's foolish not to make sure every burglar out there knows that plenty of police cars are driving through the neighborhood. Unmarked cars have their uses, but preventing burglaries is not one of them.

Beyond this, helicopters are as important to law enforcement agencies as horses are to the Royal Canadian Mounted Police. They're similar in the way that they help officers get to locations where four-wheel vehicles will not go. Having had a helicopter of my own, I know of the tremendous visual coverage that is obtained by flying above it all. Helicopters are useful in spotting culprits either on foot or in vehicles from a good distance away, not to mention the effortless pursuits afforded by the freedom of flight. Helicopters can chase a fleeing vehicle with ease and from a safe distance, keeping group units advised of manuevers and possible dangers.

And from having been a burglar as well as a helicopter pilot, I am in the position to say that helicopters are a constant threat to anyone on the ground who is up to any kind of illegal activity. They are psychological deterrents—the mere sight of one in a parking lot or on top of a building, even without any officers in them. And when they're in operation, especially at night, with their 600-million-candlepower searchlights casting shadows of everything they see, they're deadly to a person up to no good. It doesn't take a very bright person (who is riding at night en route to a crime) to realize that the light he sees coming from the sky could place his shadow on the ground beside him...along with a few dozen police cars in a matter of seconds.

If a complaint is received at police headquarters, it is then dispatched to the proper division of officers, hopefully in the general location of the complaint that was called in. However, if ground units are busy or a distance away, a police helicopter can race across the city in nothing flat, hover above the complainant's home (if a burglary or robbery has been reported) and keep an eye on things until the ground units arrive on the scene. Then the helicopter can further assist should the culprits in question be able to evade the ground units, by reporting via radio where the culprits are running or hiding.

In the survey I asked, "Would you do burglaries

or any other crimes if you were to look up and see a police helicopter with a bright searchlight shining down looking for trouble?" A total of 93 percent stated that, if they saw a police helicopter flying over the city, they would go to a city or town that didn't have a helicopter in its patrol. It's another mind game. Police helicopters offer any city or town that has them in operation more crime-deterring protection than ten police cars with two men in each. Along with that, a helicopter with one pilot and one observer can do fifty times the visual work than ten patrol cars (with two men in each) can do, considering the area covered.

The point I'm trying to make is that if your law enforcement agency is debating whether to scrap their aerial patrol, due to rising operational costs or other problems they may be having with the program, urge them to keep the blades turning! And for any department that is debating whether to purchase a helicopter or two for police work— "Go for it." It will be the best investment your community can make to cut crime and save lives. It has the strongest psychological effect on people up to no-good.

In the city where I was arrested they had not only a helicopter (which they called PAPA II) but a plane as well (PAPA I). Now planes are good, don't get me wrong. I owned three of them during the time I was a burglar, so I know their capabilities and operating costs well. Planes, when flown by a badge, are better for moving-vehicle surveillance work, where they can follow the subject in question from a distance without detection from point A to point B, all the while updating ground units of what's happening down below. However, when it becomes necessary to get in close to a dwelling under observation, to advise the ground units of someone running or hiding, planes are limited by flight characteristics. Helicopters on the other hand, can easily fly within an eyeball's reach of the action. If your town is debating between the two (plane or helicopter), in my mind there is no contest. Helicopters, even though they are a little more expensive to operate than planes, are many times more valuable.

CHAPTER 9

RESIDENTIAL ROBBERIES

We might as well confront a reality of modern life here: sometimes burglaries turn into robberies. Burglary is when someone breaks into your residence or other dwelling without confronting anyone. Residential robbery is when someone either breaks in or just plain walks into a dwelling and confronts other people with a gun, a knife or even no weapon at all. Residential robbery can also lead to assault, kidnapping, rape, murder, etc.

Residential robberies can happen anywhere, but they usually happen where something of value is known to be present: a coin collection, antiques, jewelry. At other times residential robberies occur when culprits are simply driving through wealthy residential neighborhoods. They see expensive homes, expensive cars, and just take for granted that the owners have something of value, which in more cases than not is true.

What can you do about these "could-happen-any-time" problems? I won't mention alarms because it's obvious they're very important. And I know if I were living in a nice home, I'd want an alarm that would warn me the second someone entered my yard, giving me adequate time for defensive action. And there's the air horn alarm discussed earlier.

Beyond alarms, about the only other vitally important course of action you can take is utilizing all of the mind deterrents that I have designed and talked about throughout this book. They apply to robbers as well as burglars and will work just as well at scaring the devil out of them as anyone else.

If I were to awaken and realize someone was in my bedroom going through my closets, I would continue to pretend I was sleeping. If the robber were in the next room, however, I might say something like, "Yes, Barbara, I know what the machine gun will do to the walls," or "I'll make sure I won't shoot the kids."

I would also have a panic button attached to my alarm system—beside my bed and high enough so children couldn't hit it—that would turn on lights and bells and summon the police and scare the hell out of any intruder.

Beyond this, be very careful whom you let in your house. Is it really the plumber? Is it really the wallpaper man? Ask for identification. See if there is anything suspicious about them as you're talking to them through the screen door. Don't open the door for anybody. One of the most serious problems today is the housewife who falls for a good-looking, kind face staring at her through the door. A handsome face and a few polite kind words and a sad story quickly turn into another sad story. I've heard it over and over while taking my survey of a robber's M.O. "It gets me in every time," one said with a smile.

Ladies—and I direct this to you because you're more apt to be home during the day when these things could happen—*Don't fall for stories of any kind.* I'm hoping that many of you have already followed my advice, and now have door stickers that read: "Knock all you want...we don't answer the door." Make it a habit in your home to NEVER OPEN the door for anyone that you do not know or have not sent for. And that means *NO exceptions.* Children should be trained not to let anybody in, either. You know how friendly the generation of today has become! Along with being friendly they've also become naive, or they extend the benefit of the doubt too easily to anyone and everyone they meet, thinking they're not up to anything, or if they are, "they surely wouldn't pull it on me." Then are they surprised as hell to find a gun in their face or a knife in their gut! It can happen to anyone, by anyone and the sooner everybody realizes that, the better everybody will be able to cope with life and its problems in a much safer way.

Many of us have a habit of leaving our doors open on warm summer nights to enjoy those cooling breezes that feel so good. I know...I've done it myself. But there's only one difference between the way I did it and the way a lot of people do it. I had four dogs that, however small, would warn me of a cricket drinking from my pool. And you'd better believe after seeing hundreds of dog owners tell their dogs to "shut up and go lie down," I checked out every cry from my dogs. If you insist on leaving your doors open for those few breaths of fresh air—which could be your last—have a dog. Have an alert dog nearby, who will warn you of trouble. Otherwise the possibilities of residential robberies, and burglaries where the intruder sneaks in and creeps around (trying to snatch what he can), are much higher.

Doors that are left open while you're sitting nearby, more or less prevent the chances of burglary, through that door anyway. But with robbery? It's just what the doctor ordered. The door is wide open, and you're right there...and the thief will supply the weapon and mask. All that's left is for you to get the stuff for him, open the safe and give him the keys to your car. Sad...but true. It's what residential robberies are all about.

I strongly suggest that you either have an alarm that announces intruders just as soon as they enter your yard, or if you can't afford one, use as many of my inexpensive ideas and signs (better known as *mind deterrents*) as possible. These are serious crimes, and can only be stopped by dealing with the thief's mind.

And now, back to the survey...

If you were going to burglarize a large house, but the people were having dinner, watching TV, doing the dishes, or something else in a different part of the house, would you take the chance and try to burglarize the house anyway?

A. Sixty percent would try CREEPING around while you're in the house. Depending on how messed up on drugs a burglar is, or whether you catch him and pen him in, the degree of danger will vary from situation to situation. Under no circumstance make any moves toward the burglar. I don't care how big and tough you are, or how brave: *turn around and go the other way.* To call the police at this time in his presence would possibly put him in the position of having to try whatever is necessary to stop you. Just turn around and walk away, giving him a few minutes to leave. Then call the police. It's like living in rattlesnake country. If you look down and see a rattlesnake a few feet away about to strike on one side, and your gun is lying on the ground on the other side, your first move isn't for the gun. Your first move is to get out of his striking distance and maybe he'll just leave. But if you reach for the gun, you'll quickly learn his lightning speed beats yours every time. Save yourself first, then take active measures.

Have you ever gone to a home to do a burglary, seen something inside that you had to have, but the people were home, so you turned it into an armed robbery, holding up anybody in the residence?

A. I'm afraid that this is going to be the trend of residential crimes in the future. It has been the trend for the past who knows how many years, as armed robbers would go into banks and stores and leave with fists full of dollars. For the past several years or so, the small convenience stores have been getting hit in unbelievable numbers, resulting in the deaths of both robbers and store operators alike. It is a very dangerous situation and one which will take some careful studying to solve. However, a good percentage of convenience store robbers are being caught for a mere twenty-five or fifty dollars, and getting life sentences in prison. Some are beginning to realize that, given the risk of getting caught versus the proceeds gained, it makes more sense hitting the homes of doctors, lawyers and other wealthy people. Consequently, it's more important now than ever to make sure your home is secure.

Forty-three percent stated that they have turned meant-to-be burglaries into armed robberies. If you remember, 50 percent stated that they carried weapons while doing burglaries, so this fits in.

You're in a person's bedroom and either have a gun or find theirs. They come home early and catch you in there and

approach you. Are you going to give up
or shoot the people?

A. Seventy-five percent said that if you
didn't back up and get out of their way
they'd shoot you—with your own gun, if
they had to. Remember that 50 percent
said they carried weapons. But now when
asked how many would shoot you, we have
75 percent. That's 25 percent more, or half
of those who don't carry guns. Where are
they going to get the guns to shoot you
with? How about the gun on your bed table, or under your bed? Guns that are not
hidden could be used on you and, if not
you, when stolen they could be used on
someone else. Hide your guns—yes, even
in your own home. It only takes a minute
and could save a life.

CHAPTER 10

HOMEOWNER'S DEFENSE PLAN (For each of Burglar's Offensive Steps)

I've spent a lot of space in this book emphasizing mind games, mental deterrents that will make most burglars too concerned about their own safety to break into your home. I can't overemphasize the importance of these mental deterrents. Everything I saw and learned as a burglar, and everything I've heard from the other inmates here in prison have totally convinced me that mind games are the most effective way to make your home safe.

And so to conclude this book I'm going to put all this in mental perspective.

Now I'm going to explain to you the three steps a burglar goes through while hitting a residence. Keep in mind that these are called *steps*. For each offensive *step*, I will give you the defensive *plan* to counteract his steps. These are the *mind games.* The burglar's overall objective is to get in, get your possessions, and get out safely, without being seen if possible. Burglary along with every other residential crime is a conceptual process, carried out through mental commands that can best be prevented by mind deterrents. Once you know this and believe in this, you are on the road to a safer home and longer lasting possessions.

STEP ONE consists of THE BURGLAR'S INITIAL VISUAL CONTACT WITH A RESIDENCE OR OTHER DWELLING HE INTENDS TO HIT. He processes all available information: whether, from a distance, it looks as if anybody's home; whether he has any place to hide while attempting to gain entry. Bushes, cars and solid fences are only a few of the things that offer him protective coverage. Is there anybody out and about from nearby houses that could possibly see him, thwarting his goals? Is there a good place to run if something goes wrong? Does the place look like it has anything of value? What kind of windows and doors does it have, and will it be easy to get into? These are a few of the things that go through a burglar's mind in the initial seconds of his visual contact with your home.

Try to picture this mentally right now. Imagine for a moment that *you're* the burglar, approaching *your* home.

Now is the time to try PLAN ONE. The first part of *plan one* is to give the burglar as little help as possible. Remember the newspapers on the lawn or driveway, the mail sticking out of the mailbox, the city's garbage containers still sitting in front of the house, the name plate on the side of your residence or mailbox, showing everyone your name, exact address, etc., that little note tacked to the front door blowing in the wind saying "open for burglary," the hanging advertisement crammed in the door slot, the hanging samples on the door-knob. All these have got to go. They are the signs he is looking for. Along with plan one—removing these items—is removing other items that might attract him. Is your garage door open, exposing all your valuable tools, bicycles, lawn furniture, chain saws, or are these things just sitting on your front lawn? These are things that will attract burglars like flies. Did your son forget to bring in the lawn-mower last night? Again, you are advertising to anybody that this stuff is free for the taking. So plan one is to REMOVE IF POSSIBLE ANY INVI-TATIONS TO HIT YOUR PLACE.

Beyond this, there is the matter of someone being at home. Even if there isn't, you want the burglar to think there is. This is a matter of lights on timers, a stereo turned on, a dog barking. If it seems that someone is home, you'll stop some bur-glars. They'll go to another house. But 60 percent of the inmates said they would hit a house with someone in it. This means that if they think they can get in and creep around without being caught...they will. It doesn't mean that they're just going to march in the front door, walk past you and lug the stuff out. But at this stage of the game—the burglar's step one—there is nothing you can do to stop him if he's decided to enter whether or not you're home. When he gets closer...Yes! You will have a better opportunity.

If the burglar proceeds to STEP TWO, he enters

your yard, first giving a quick glance to everything within ten feet of the house. The second time around he'll scan more closely for anything that looks threatening. Now it is important that you understand that the second *step* a burglar takes is to CHECK OUT YOUR RESIDENCE FOR ANY SIGNS OF THINGS THAT SEEM THREATENING.

So PLAN TWO involves CONVINCING THE BURGLAR THAT YOURS IS THE MOST THREATENING HOUSE HE COULD POSSIBLY ENTER—deploying mind games implying that all kinds of strange things could happen if he messes with your place— so maybe it would be better if he went elsewhere. Why not just tell him that? I made a sign for a small New England–style barn I built in my backyard in Florida, which had all of my tools and motorcycles and other valuables in it. The sign read, "Dear Burglars, this building has multiple alarms. Why waste your time here, when you could be working on my neighbor's house?" They had alarms too, so it was a waste of time there anyway.

I can't stress too much the role that simple little notes can play in deterring a burglar. Even if you're lazy, you can take a few minutes to scrawl a few of these.

Here's a note that could be printed up on a six-by-eight-inch card and displayed in various locations to the rear of the home. It's designed more or less for application on the inside of sliding glass doors where it won't attract attention by blowing in the wind. From an ex-burglar's point of view, and using only an ounce of common sense, this combination of words, seen by a person from the outside of your home, would stop anyone from breaking into your residence. The note could read something like this:

"Sandy... Roger's rattlesnakes have gotten loose again and are somewhere in the house. They haven't been fed now for some time, so please don't bother feeding the cat tonight as they are extremely dangerous. The police have been called."

As I've just mentioned, one of the burglar's *steps* is to walk around the dwelling he plans on hitting before he actually pronounces the place safe enough to hit. More than likely he will run into this sign if it's displayed on the inside of a sliding glass door or on the inside window of a regular door. As soon as he sees it, I'd almost guarantee that he won't mess with your residence. For mobile homes, one could be made up for each front and back door in about five minutes. And again they will do more than any lock ever could.

Here's another sign, for people who live in places where they can't have dogs—and where that fact is advertised on a sign at the office:

"Dottie...Never mind the ironing tonight. Tom brought his Doberman over for a couple of days even though he wasn't supposed to, because it's gone wild or something and bitten two people near his home."

Stupid, right? I agree. But I'll bet you no one would dare enter that house. Here's another:

"Marge...You were right, Fred's Pit Bull does have rabies, but the doctor has given him a shot and he's not very gentle tonight, so disregard feeding. He's inside sleeping."

You should be able to think of many others by now. There are still other things to do as part of *plan two*. Remember the two-foot-in-diameter dog's dishes, maybe sitting by both back door and front door. And how about the ATTACK DOGS sign, and (perhaps) one of those two- or three-foot bones they have for large dogs to play with. Don't forget those alarm stickers on all doors and windows, telling him that, as soon as he enters the home, alarms will sound.

Believe me, these work.

Part of *step two* for the burglar who won't go in if you're home also involves knocking on the door and ringing the bell. Sometimes I used to take a plant from a neighbor's house, and place it in front of the door. If someone answered, they thought they had received a gift, and didn't get too suspicious. That way at least I could come back another time and try again.

So the burglar knocks. But what good is it? The sign says that you don't answer your door. Then he tries to look in your windows, but he can't because you and your family have learned how to close the curtains properly so that there's not even a tiny place he can see in. On top of all this, there's either a TV or stereo playing inside when you're out, giving him the general impression that someone is home. By this time if he is still around, he is totally confused, messed up, doesn't know which house to try next—the one on the right or the one on the left. But he does know one thing. This house has too many things wrong to mess with, and he's moving on.

If he's crazy enough to continue—and my personal opinion is that even if he's messed up on drugs he is going to leave by this time—he will now put STEP THREE into effect and take out his tools. If he didn't bring any, he'll use the ones you left in the garden the night before, or the hammer you used to fix that gutter three days ago and forgot to put away. Now believe me, the ruggedness of your locks and the length of your deadbolts are not doing to do a damn thing to deter him if he's already pushed all of these other *mind games* aside. I've come upon many of the best locks in the trade and there's not one of them that can hold up against the leverage of a three-foot crowbar that forces the door against the one-inch bolt extending into the wall.

Take it for granted that he is in now. And his next move is going to be looking for the valuables that interest him the most. If this is one of the burglars who falls in the 63 percent category of cutting phone lines, the police will be en route at this time or already have the house surrounded— if you have a leased-line alarm system, or if the phone company would put into effect the system that I mentioned earlier. The survey showed that the most valuable, most commonly sought items are, first, money, and then jewelry. HIS SEARCH FOR THESE ITEMS IS PART OF *STEP THREE*.

Now PLAN THREE goes into effect: TO CURB HIS PROFIT GAIN AS MUCH AS POSSIBLE. Again we bring in a few mind games to counteract his offensive moves. As seen in the survey, the first place a burglar looks is the master bedroom. I did the same. Why? Because the top drawer of the lady's dresser always has the jewelry lying in some kind of special velvet rollup container or jewelry box, or one of those round, zippered, cotton pouches with silk linings. Sometimes, the same containers are hidden in the next drawer down, mixed in with the bras or slipped in a cashmere sweater. But all burglars check out every single drawer in your bedroom and then, shortly afterwards, everything with a cabinet door on it. *Never* put anything that can't be replaced easily, anything with sentimental or financial value, in either drawers or cabinets. If you do, then you might as well accept that one day they could be gone.

After the burglar has wiped out the lady's dresser, he goes to the man's dresser, finding a similar situation. Sure it's convenient to have what you wear every day of the week sitting right in front of you, but today's way of life won't permit that.

Plan three entails THE CONCEALMENT OF YOUR EXPENSIVE JEWELRY AND LARGE AMOUNTS OF CASH IN THE BEST WAY POSSIBLE. If you're wealthy... it's a safe. If you're not wealthy, it's a hollowed-out book or another of the hiding places summarized in Chapter 5. There are several good places to conceal jewelry, cash, medication and coins, but most people today are too lazy to take the time to bother hiding things and then retrieve them when needed.

There have been many deterrents discussed throughout this book. They have been commented on by me, and by the other inmates. It is very important to realize that, no matter what you yourself think about these conclusions, they are a measure of what's happening out there in the criminal world. These conclusions have come from men in prison, imprisoned for the crimes of burglary and robbery. Remember these questions have been given to criminal minds, not to or by the people of crime-prevention programs, whose material is derived from the statistics of crime. As I've said in the past: if it's a toothache, it's the dentist. If it's a clogged toilet, it's the plumber. And for remedies for crimes: there's nobody who can help you better than people who have done them. The problem is getting them to do this while they're still on the wrong side of the fence. That's what I was able to do while in prison.

I've presented problem after problem, situation after situation, and for the most part, given you strategies for dealing with them. Now the choice is yours to evaluate your findings and take preventive measures, so that you will be safe from residential crimes.

I would like, in closing, to explain the effects this book will have on some of you. I think about the best way I can do this is to remind you of a fairly recent "crazy idea" that worked. Remember a few years back when there was an item around called the Pet Rock. Can't you just hear the inventor trying to tell one of his friends that he'd come up with a new idea that would net millions yet cost nothing to produce. And when asked what that might be, he'd reply, "Oh, just an old ordinary rock with the word 'pet' in front of it."

How many of you would have thought the guy was crazy? How many of you would have laughed at the combination of words "pet" and "rock," thinking it never could have been a sales success?

Well, whatever the number is, it's the same percentage of people who won't utilize these mind games and signs—even though they'll do what they're meant to do, IF GIVEN THE CHANCE. My methods require your belief at least until you put them to use. Then whether you believe them or not isn't important. The burglars will and that's what counts. It's hard to picture a place if you haven't been there before, just as it's probably hard for you to understand how these simple little signs—these simple little clever word combinations—could deter a burglar.

I wonder how many cynics there'll be who doubt these ideas and conclusions, how many people who have read this book will say to themselves or others, "Are you kidding me, you don't think a few clever signs stuck here and there, a few large dog's dishes and a three-foot bone is going to stop crime—do you?"

I have given you some very powerful advice in this book. Try taking the time and interest to correct the situations around your home that make it look like a classified ad for burglars. Try using all of the *mind* deterrents I've suggested. Then your chances of becoming one of the statistics will be greatly reduced, if not totally gone.

I know that some of my ideas sound crazy. I know that some of my signs leave some of you doubting. But can't you see...that's what they're supposed to do: leave you, the person who is reading them—whether good guy or bad guy—wondering about them. It's that shadow of doubt that will make burglars go elsewhere. Words are powerful, sometimes more powerful than a gun or other form of physical offense. The sooner you realize that the only way to control undesirables outside your door or window is with words (frightening words offering danger to their well-being) and other *mind games,* the sooner the burglary statistics will go down.

Then there are the others, who will do what I have suggested. They'll take the active measures they need to, and do away with anything that advertises their absence. They'll stick up their signs and then, later, when they're not as concerned about crime prevention as they once were, their defenses will get sloppy. They'll forget closing the curtains, they'll mount on the fence that new name sign their son made in school. The old fight-crime attitude will fade away into the night, and the oh-it-will-never-happen-to-us feeling will start to take over. Remember, not only is residential crime prevention like a combination lock in the respect of having the *right* deterrents (numbers, for the lock) but it's also like the combination lock in the sense that, in order to prevent residential crimes and keep preventing them, you need to utilize *all* of the mind deterrents as a lock requires *all* of its numbers before it will open.

It would only take, at most, one day to clean up your home and property of any advertising situations and to display the stickers and signs.

Try it.

The burglar has nothing but time.

You have everything to lose.

Superthief Jack MacLean will be leading special seminars on crime prevention for law enforcement agencies. In addition, any organization which is interested in having Superthief speak to their group may write for information to:

Superthief Crime Prevention Program
949 North Kings Road
Suite 114
Los Angeles, California